"Lynelle Mason's characters come alive as she spins this historical fiction tale of N.W.'s exploits aboard *The Anne* and as a participant in Georgia's first settlement. As a Georgia native, I was pleased to discover the thoroughness of her research and how she interwove facts into her inspiring story. Young readers will be informed about Georgia's early days and challenged by N.W.'s adventures."

—Sue Sisson
Retired School Social Worker

"Lynelle Mason, a gifted storyteller and lover of history, easily engages young readers in her works of historical fiction. The challenges and adventures of young N.W. Jones continue *in Trailblazer, Part Two* as he transitions from his teenage years into young adulthood within the British colony of Georgia. Readers of all ages will enjoy this fact-filled tale about life during an important time in our homeland's evolution into a nation."

—Jeanne H. Baucom
Hospice Chaplain

"Lynelle Mason has a talent for making history real. Through her craftsmanship the history of Georgia comes alive for all ages."

—Joan Trundle
Retired Elementary School Teacher

"Lynelle Mason has written an informative and thoughtful historical novel of early Georgia. Viewed through the eyes and actions of young N.W. Jones, readers experience the trials of growing up and pursuing a profession in a young and raw colony."

—*Jim Garrett*
Special Education Resource Teacher

"*Trailblazer, Part Two* continues the exciting adventures of young N.W. Jones and his dream of becoming a doctor in colonial Georgia. Readers of *Trailblazer, Part One* will be delighted to have a chance to follow N.W.'s further struggles as a young adult to achieve his goal, while new readers will be readily captivated by this engaging historical novel."

—*Verbie Lovorn Prevost*
Professor of American Literature

"While residing in Atlanta, I made a number of business and pleasure trips to Savannah without giving thought to how Savannah began as a colony. *Trailblazer* by Lynelle Sweat Mason provides insight into the early history of Savannah and its settlers. They faced angry seas, sickness, disease, hunger, a mecurial environment, the unknown, and even death. They did this with courage and determination to make it a new world for themselves and future generations. Well done, Lynelle!"

—*Ron Cooper*
Retired Information Technology Executive

Trailblazer

PART TWO

*

A TRILOGY BY

LYNELLE SWEAT MASON

© 2017
Published in the United States by Nurturing Faith Inc., Macon GA,
www.nurturingfaith.net.

Library of Congress Cataloging-in-Publication Data is available.

ISBN 978-1-63528-026-5

Dedication
To my dynamic trio,
Timothy Rodrigues, Janet Haney, and Alan Mason,
who are relentless in their efforts to publicize my books

In Appreciation
To all my book lovers at
Alexian Village,
First Baptist Church of Chattanooga,
Walker County Retired Teachers Association,
and friends and family far and near:
Many of you buy every book I write.
For you I am most grateful.

Contents

The Georgia where N.W. lived as a teenager and young man (1740–1753) was marked by wars and Indian turmoil. The "Malcontents" finally succeeded in getting the laws against rum and slaves repealed. General James Oglethorpe was fed up with their gripes, so he returned to England. The trustees also grew tired of the endless complaints and decided to turn the colony over to the British government. Georgia was now a crown colony.

CHAPTER 1

Growing Pains

Noble Wimberly Jones was out for a brisk morning walk when he tripped over a rotten plank near Georgia's crumbling courthouse. He glanced down at his ever-growing feet, hoping no one saw him sprawled on the dirt. N.W. frowned, muttering to himself, "Our courthouse is decaying, yet we have money to wage war against Spain. What a dreadful time to turn 16!"

After dusting himself off, N.W. resumed his walk. It wasn't long before he spied his best friend John coming from the opposite direction, all decked out in his army attire.

N.W. threw his arms into the air. "Hello, John. Or, should I address you as Captain Milledge? You look great. What's going on these days with you and your family?"

John slapped his hands against his thighs and winked. "So far we have a roof over our heads, and no one is complaining about going hungry." His face became somber. "N.W., you seem worried. What's bothering you?"

N.W. frowned. "Why does growing up have to be so complicated?"

John rolled his eyes. "I guess that's the price we pay in becoming adults."

N.W. looked down and ground his boot into the dirt. "Until recently everything I thought and did was connected to becoming Georgia's best doctor."

John wrinkled his brow. "Is that no longer true?"

"Oh, yes, it's still true. It's just that other things keep trying to put a lid on my plans."

John shrugged his shoulders. "Does this by any chance have to do with you turning 16 and a war with Spain on the horizon?"

N.W. pinched himself. "Ouch! You're disturbing my pot of worries. I personally see this war with Spain as a stumbling block on my path toward becoming a full-fledged doctor." In a half-whisper he added, "Do you remember me telling you about my last talk with Dr. Nunis?"

John sneered. "Yeah. When he told you the Spaniards would whip us." John grabbed N.W.'s arm. "You're not doubting our war with Spain, are you? If you are, then you're not thinking straight. We really don't have a choice. If we do nothing, the Spaniards will gobble us up and slowly make their way up the eastern coast. One by one our English colonies will vanish. We simply can't let that happen!"

N.W. stood tall with his hands clenched. He nodded. "You're right. However, when I try to sleep I find my mind filled with hundreds of Spaniards and Englishmen maimed and dying." He dug his foot into Savannah's sandy soil. "What if I become a soldier? When the battle is over will I ever be free to study, learn, and practice medicine?"

John impatiently waved off N.W.'s objections. "Long before you and I were born, Spain claimed that the land we live on belongs to that country. England disagrees and says we have a right to live here." John paused and crossed his arm. "Right now we've a battle to fight. If we don't win, nothing else is going to matter. I suggest you start thinking less about yourself and more about the rest of us." He gave N.W. a friendly poke in his ribs. "By the way, your father is looking for you."

"Thanks for the warning. I'll hurry home." N.W. grinned. "As you know, Father doesn't like to be kept waiting."

When N.W. was halfway home his path collided with his father's. "There you are! I've been scrounging the neighborhood looking for you. If my recollections serve me well, today is your birthday. It's time you and I make a visit to the Trustees Store to get you fitted up in your military finery. How does that sound to you?"

Taking a firm hold of Father's arm, N.W. said: "Wait, Father. We need to talk."

Father raised his eyebrows. "What's bothering you?"

N.W. began wringing his hands. "You asked how I felt about getting my uniform." His voice weakened. Finally he blurted, "Father, I'm afraid! I know this war with Spain must be fought, and I'm willing to do my share of the fighting." He paused. Looking at Father with begging eyes, he continued, "But you know me. I dream of healing instead of killing."

Father reached over and gave N.W. a bear hug. "I do understand and care about your feelings. I wish we could solve our problems without going to war. But with every day that passes, a new crisis between our countries erupts."

The two of them sat silently for several minutes. Finally Father spoke. His voice was strong. "When we begin fighting we'll need you to serve in our medical corps. You'll be busy day and night."

N.W. sighed. "But, Father I don't know a thing about . . ."

Father waved off N.W.'s objections. "We can talk later. Right now we need to get you fitted up."

N.W. gulped and gave Father a mock salute. "Yes, sir. Lead the way. Cadet Jones is ready to join in the defense of Georgia." The two of them strolled over to the Trustees Store.

"Hello, Master Jones," said the storekeeper. "What can I do for you today?"

Father squared his shoulders and took charge. "We're here to get N.W.'s military . . ."

N.W. put a firm hand on Father's shoulder, saying, "Pardon me. Don't you think it's time I began speaking for myself?"

Father sheepishly stepped back and gave deference to N.W.

"Sir," said N.W., "I turned 16 today and I'm here to get my uniform and my soldiering equipment."

The storekeeper smiled. "Excuse me for a few minutes. I'll be right back." Soon he returned, bearing a bundle of pants and jackets. "Here, try these on and we'll go from there."

The first pair of pants was way too short. They dangled below N.W.'s knees. Father muffled a laugh, saying, "Those might have worked five years ago."

The second pair was way too long. N.W. bobbled his head sideways. "Sir," he inquired, "do you have a pair where the length is somewhere between the first and second pair?" Flustered, the storekeeper rushed back to his supply closet. He was gone for a long time, but when he returned he had a pair that fit N.W. as if they'd been made especially for him.

The storekeeper stepped back a few paces and then squinted his eyes. "Now to find you a jacket . . . that will be a little easier I'm thinking. You're about my size, but you'll need a little growing room."

With his uniform and gear in tow, N.W. thanked the storekeeper and returned home with Father. N.W. quickly excused himself and turned to go to his attic quarters.

Father tugged on N.W.'s arm. "Wait a minute. I've one more important matter to take care of before you don your uniform and go promenading around the square."

N.W. ran his hands through his hair. "What's so urgent, Father?"

Father quietly retrieved his cherished pocket watch, saying, "Sit here beside me. Since you were a tiny lad you've been fascinated by my watch. Today, N.W., on your 16th birthday I'm entrusting it to you. My father gave me this watch when I turned 16. His father had passed it on to him." Father placed the watch into N.W.'s hands and clasped his hands over it. "As long as you keep this watch you'll carry with you a vital part of the Jones family, past and present. When your firstborn son turns 16, I trust you'll pass it on to him for safekeeping."

Tears trickled down N.W.'s cheeks. He spoke in whispered tones. "This reminds me of the time when we were on our way to board the *Anne* and were threatened by a highwayman. Father, you were willing to give him your gold watch if he'd spare our lives. When I asked if you really would have given him the watch you said, 'Although my watch is a family heirloom I'd gladly swap it in exchange for the safety of my family.' Father, I hope I never forget that people are more important than gold and that a good name is something to always cherish."

All this time Mother had been a silent onlooker. Now she rushed over and gave N.W. a whack on his rump. "Go put on your uniform and we'll see if you can pass inspection."

N.W., clutching his prized watch and uniform, took off upstairs. Soon he returned. He gave a snappy salute, saying, "Cadet Jones, reporting for duty."

Mother threw her hands in the air. "I'm not believing this! What happened to my little boy?" She turned to Father. "I think I'll need a stick to keep the girls away."

Father laughed. "Did it occur to you that your son might like having the girls swarm around him?"

N.W. blushed. "If you don't mind, I think I'll go for a walk. I'll be home later this afternoon." N.W. made a beeline to John's house. Along the way he heard scraps of whispers from the people he passed. Soon he knocked on John's door.

John slapped himself across his cheek. "Sarah," he called to his sister, "some good-looking soldier just knocked on our door. See if you know him."

Sarah quickly laid her needlework aside and joined in giving N.W. a rousing welcome. John told N.W., "Although it galls me to say it, you do look rather stunning in your new uniform."

Sarah urged, "Let's go outside. I want to show you off."

It wasn't long before a crowd of girls encircled N.W. and John, clamoring for attention.

N.W. kept running his fingers under his collar, but he couldn't help smiling. He enjoyed being adored.

A cute little redhead with bouncy curls and an obvious Irish brogue pushed her way through the crowd until she was within earshot of Sarah. N.W. bent his ear, hoping to hear what she'd say.

The lass cupped her hand against her mouth and whispered, "My heart is racing like a cheetah's. Who is that handsome soldier with you?"

N.W. politely stepped back, pretending he hadn't heard a word. The girls continued talking.

"He's N.W. Jones, the eldest son of Noble Jones."

"Will you introduce us?"

"Sure. Just remember he's shy around girls. If you want to get him talking, say something about medicine."

The girl playfully slapped Sarah's arm. "You're teasing me, aren't you?"

"No. N.W. is already known for his medical skills. He studied with Doctor Nunis until the doctor left the colony. Come with me and I'll introduce the two of you."

"N.W., " said Sarah, "I'd like for you to meet Kathleen, a friend of mine."

"Hello, Kathleen," said N.W. "Sarah chooses her friends wisely. I like your Irish brogue and pretty red hair."

N.W. looked on while Kathleen flung her hands across her heart and opened her mouth. Instead of speaking she began giggling. Pretty soon all the girls were giggling.

John stepped forward and pulled N.W. aside. "Girls," said John, shaking his head, "for the life of me I can't figure them out."

Scratching his head, N.W. said, "Me neither. Why are all of them giggling?"

John laughed. "I've been told that girls do that when they're stricken over the good looks of a young man." He grinned. "Why they're doing it over the likes of you dumfounds me."

"Oh," whispered N.W. He turned and gave Sarah a hug and said to John, "Keep me posted on any new developments with those blasted Spaniards."

Before returning home N.W. stopped by Mary's place at the trading post.

Mary beamed. "Hello, handsome soldier. How are you?"

With a pained look, N.W. asked, "Do you really want to know?"

Mary grasped N.W.'s shaking hands and steadied them. N.W. looked into her eyes. "Mary, it's just a matter of time before we go to war against the Spanish." He squirmed. "I'm scared! I don't know a thing about doctoring wounded men."

Mary fastened her eyes on N.W. "Try not to worry. You'll do fine. Only liars say they aren't afraid during a war."

N.W sported a half-grin. "This soldier best be on his way home. At least I know I'm not a liar."

For the next several weeks N.W., along with the other male colonists, daily practiced his marching and shooting skills while waiting for some provoking action by the Spanish. It got so that N.W. felt as if he was holding a cannon ball that might explode at any minute.

In November of 1739 Father rushed home with some disturbing news. "It's happened!" he cried, trying to catch his breath. He repeated the same words over and over.

N.W. shook Father, saying, "Calm down and tell us what dreadful thing has befallen us."

Wringing his hands, Father blurted: "It's the Spaniards. They laid an ambush and killed two of our Scots on Amelia Island. General Oglethorpe will strike back on them with vengeance."

N.W. bit his lower lip to keep from bursting into tears.

CHAPTER 2

Days of Reckoning

1740

N.W listened intently as Father struggled to control his emotions. "On New Years Day," Father said, "I'll leave for Frederica to assist General Oglethorpe and a group of soldiers scouting for Spanish forts along the St. John's River."

"Father, will I be going?"

"No, not this time. I'll feel better knowing you're here taking care of Mother and your siblings and making sure no unwanted visitors break through our waterways."

N.W. caught Mother's eye and winked. "I'll do my best to keep Mother from misbehaving. When will you return?"

"We probably won't be gone much more than a week," said Father. "If you need anything, contact the Marines stationed at Fort Wimberly."

While Father was out scouting for Spanish forts N.W. spent many hours teaching Mother and his younger sister, Mary, how to fire a musket. Mother never seemed to catch on, but Mary was a fast learner. "Holy mackerel, Mary! Your aim is better than many of our recruits. I pity the fellow that challenges you."

The week passed quickly, and soon N.W. joined the crowd welcoming Father back from his scout-finding mission. Without giving him time to sit down, N.W. began peppering Father with questions. "Before you left you were distraught; now you're bubbling with enthusiasm. What happened?"

"We hadn't gone far before our Indian fighters burned the Spanish Fort Picolata," said Father. "Before the day ended, Fort St. Francis surrendered to us. We captured all their artillery and ammunition." Father paused. "Do you mind if I have a seat?"

N.W. blushed. "Excuse me, Father. Please sit. You know me. I get carried away at times. Please go on."

"Soon General Oglethorpe will go before the Carolina legislature and ask for troop support. He'll also seek the help of the British Navy in setting up a blockade against St. Augustine. I've been put in charge of our Creek and Indian fighters."

Father grabbed N.W. by the shoulder and looked him in the eye. "We're ready to chase the Spanish to the city gate of St. Augustine. N.W., are you prepared to do your part?"

N.W. felt his throat close, and for a moment he was silent. "Yes, I'm ready," he whispered. When Father left to check in with the Marines stationed at Fort Wimberly, N.W. asked his mother, "Can I tell you something?"

Mother took one look at his worried brow and responded, "This secret is between you and me only. Go ahead."

N.W. threw his hands into the air. "I feel so helpless! I know next to nothing about treating someone who has been shot, much less someone wounded by a bayonet. What am I going to do?"

Mother paused and put her fist under her chin. She spoke softly. "Son, your natural instincts will carry you through this ordeal. In the end I guess you'll have to do the best you can and leave the rest to the Almighty."

N.W. sighed, nodding his head. "I knew you'd understand." He hesitated before saying, "There's something else laying heavy on my mind. I've tried so hard to blot Doctor Nunis out of my mind, but he refuses to leave. He's been gone from Savannah more than a year, but every day I think of him. It was just after the Spanish beheaded two of our soldiers on Amelia Island that he sat me down and told me a chilling story."

N.W. paused but Mother urged him to continue. "The same day Chief Tomochichi died I stopped by to see Doctor Nunis. He was tossing his clothes and medicine into a small trunk. I asked him why he was in such a hurry to leave. When he answered, his hands were trembling and his speech garbled. 'I'm leaving Savannah very soon,' he said. 'I need to get as far away from the Spanish as I can.'"

I asked him why he was so fearful of the Spanish. He told me that long ago he got in trouble with the Catholic authorities in Portugal. He managed to trick them and secured passage to London and from London to Georgia. They swore they'd get even with him. He was afraid if the Spanish won the battle against Georgia, they'd come looking for him."

"General Oglethorpe and my father are certain we'll win," I assured him. "Why are you so certain Spain will beat us?"

"Doctor Nunis caught his breath and then said, 'Believe me, N.W., I hope with all my heart I'm wrong. The Castillo de San Marcos has been bombarded many times but has never been captured!'"

N.W. took Mother by the hand. "What if Doctor Nunis is right and Father is wrong? Mother, what if the battle drags on and on?"

Mother, wearing a deep frown, said nothing. In a little while N.W. excused himself and left to join the other cadets at the practice range.

At dusk that same day N.W. returned home. Slowly he kicked off his boots and in a monotonous voice said, "Every day we march around Johnson Square and practice musket drills." N.W. wiped away the grime he'd acquired while marching and began mimicking the drill sergeant's commands. "Unlock your musket, retrieve the gun powder, rip it open and pour it down the barrel, grab your ramrod and push the powder to the bottom of the barrel, put your ramrod up, aim, and fire!"

Father laughed. "I hear you're making good progress. What would you say to becoming the medical assistant for General Oglethorpe?"

"You shouldn't tease me with such foolishness, Father," said N.W. "Who ever heard of a cadet serving as a personal valet to a general?"

Father shrugged his shoulders and smiled. "I'm just repeating what General Oglethorpe told me. If you're not interested, I'll tell him to pick someone else."

N.W. grabbed Father's arm. "Hold on, Father. I'm honored and very interested. Did he say why he wanted me?"

"Yes," said Father, "Oglethorpe remembers the kind words Doctor Nunis shared with him concerning your potential as a physician."

N.W. shot a worried glance toward Mother. "How do I go about taking care of a general who shares every hardship made by his enlisted men?"

"You take care of a general the same way you take care of any patient," said Mother. "General Oglethorpe, since he thinks he's immune to sickness, will defy your patience. Can you stand up to him?"

N.W. nodded his head. Seconds later, without any warning, he fell asleep on the kitchen floor. Mother covered him with a quilt and propped a pillow under his head.

The month of May broke through the hovering war clouds, bringing good news for N.W.

One day Father returned home from work early and declared, "It's moving day! Let's gather our belongings and be on our way. Our new home, Wormsloe, is waiting for us to move in."

N.W. joined the waiting crew of Marines and helped them transfer the family's belongings to Wormsloe. At last the job was finished and N.W. was free to investigate his new home.

"Father," said N.W., "the house is beautiful. I'm amazed. The last time I was here you had only the outer walls and bastions in place."

Father reached for Mother's hand and whispered, "How do you like it?"

Mother pinched herself. "Am I dreaming, or is this for real?"

Father plastered her with love pats. "Darling, it's for real!"

Mother laid her head on Father's chest. "I've always known you were smart, but this is mind-boggling. Honey, how did you go about building Wormsloe?"

N.W. and Mary listened as Father waxed eloquent. "I learned about building materials from the Marines who have traveled to St. Augustine. The houses there are made out of tabby, a mixture of sand and seashells. My crew of Marines has been working feverishly on our new house for the past two years. It still isn't completely built. We'll be adding an upper one-half to it later on, and we'll also be building a screened porch that will cover three sides of our house. Come; let's all of us go inside."

When Mother walked into the kitchen she clapped her hands and danced a little jig. Her plaited ash brown hair, now bearing white streaks, came unbound and tumbled down her shoulders.

N.W. pointed to the H-shaped fireplace. "Look, Mother, there's a fireplace on the outside as well as one in your kitchen." He sniffed the air. "I can smell a pot of coffee brewing. Can you?"

Mary peeped inside a door leading from the kitchen. "What's this?" she asked.

Before Father could answer, Inigo, wanting to get his share of attention, began rolling around on the brick tiled floor. Father made his best funny face, saying, "It must be for storing Mary's caterpillars."

Inigo had triggered Mother's giggle box. The more Mother tried to stop giggling, the more pronounced it became. Soon Mary joined Mother.

N.W. winked at Father. "Women! I'll never understand them. How about you, Father?"

"No," replied Father, "but I don't aim to stop trying. This is a storage room for such things as flour, sugar, and spices. The other storage room is for honey, sorghum, fruits, and vegetables. "

Father tapped Inigo on his shoulder. "Mary will have her own room, and so will you and N.W."

After Father had shown the children their rooms N.W. said, "Let's go outside. I'm anxious for you to tell us about the wall around our house and the places you've built where we can defend ourselves if we're attacked."

"There is a thick wall that surrounds the house, making it very hard for intruders to break through. There are four bastions from which you can fire weapons," said Father.

N.W. looked on as Mary, standing with her jaw squared and her pretend gun hoisted, repeated the steps N.W. had taught her with perfect cadence.

"Good for you, Mary," said N.W. "It makes me feel better about having to leave when I know you can discharge your weapon, if you must."

N.W. checked his timepiece. "Holy mackerel! I need to leave for musket practice. I'll stay over tonight at Savannah. I'll see you all sometime tomorrow."

In his Savannah house, after musket and marching drills, N.W. found a package addressed to him. He wasted no time opening it. His eyes fell on a sheaf of papers bearing the title: "Treating Battle Wounds."

There were also many vials of medicine for treating malaria and similar symptoms. Swallowing hard, N.W. whispered: "Good for you, Doctor Nunis. At least when I go into battle I'll know a little about treating wounds."

N.W. put on a pot of coffee, lit a candle, and sat down to read. At midnight he was still drinking coffee and reading. When he finally went to sleep he was bombarded in his dreams by a group of screaming soldiers, gushing with blood and tugging on his arm. They were begging for help.

N.W. woke in the early hours of morning, drenched in sweat and wringing his hands. He steadied himself on the edge of his mattress and released a long sigh. "I'll do the best I can and hope the Almighty comes to my rescue."

N.W. gulped down some coffee, slipped into his trousers and tunic, packed up the goods from Doctor Nunis in his knapsack, and hustled to find someone to give him a ride to Wormsloe.

CHAPTER 3

A Battle Plan Gone Awry

Castillo de San Marcos
1740

N.W. lifted the lid from the simmering pot over the hearth fire. "Ah," he said, sniffing the hearty flavors of beef mixed with onions, potatoes, and carrots. Smacking his lips, he gave Mother a quick hug. "I'm famished! All those marching and musket drills have worn me out." He sniffed the air a second time. "There's no mistake about that aroma. It has to be coffee!"

After supper N.W. began probing Father for answers. "Why is it taking General Oglethorpe so long to launch this battle?" He scratched his right ear. "It's been five months since the Spanish beheaded two of our soldiers on Amelia Island."

Father rocked back and forth on his feet. "I can tell you one thing. It isn't General Oglethorpe's fault. He's an incurable optimist."

N.W. raised his eyebrows. "So?"

Father bent over, making eye contact with N.W. "Oglethorpe's big problem has been convincing the Carolina legislature to support our effort. General Oglethorpe began in January asking for their help." He paused and placed his arm on N.W.'s shoulder. "Finally they've agreed to assist us. However, it's taken a commander of His Majesty's Royal Navy and a personal loan from Oglethorpe to convince the Carolinians." Father winked. "The Carolinians don't seem too eager to fight the Spanish."

N.W. fixed his gaze on Father. "Does General Oglethorpe really believe we can beat the Spanish?"

"Yes, he does," said Father. "Oglethorpe believes the Spanish will surrender their town and fort rather than fight us."

N.W. shrugged his shoulders. "No army has ever been able to take the Castillo de San Marcos. I must say our general is not lacking when it comes to confidence."

N.W. began pacing the floor. He was frowning. "Your news sounds as if we might be leaving soon."

Father's voice softened. "It won't be long."

A couple of weeks passed. One evening as the sun was sinking behind the horizon Father arrived home. "I can tell by the look on your face you have big news," said N.W. "What is it?"

Father's voice grew strong. "This morning after my mail delivery to Frederica, General Oglethorpe and I talked. It seems Carolina needs 30 more men to complete their regiment. You and I have been assigned to help fill their quota. Captain Peter Laffite of Purrysburg, Carolina, will be our leader. I'll be serving as lieutenant in charge of a group of Creek and Cherokee Indians, and you'll be serving as a cadet and medical assistant."

N.W.'s eyes lit up. "Did General Oglethorpe really say I'd be going as a medical assistant?"

Father puffed out his chest, wearing a big grin. "I knew that would please you. Oglethorpe also said he's listing you as one of his medical advisors. How does that suit you?"

N.W. released a booming laugh. "The very thought of telling James Oglethorpe what to do makes me tremble. I take it we'll be leaving soon."

Father nodded. "When the sun begins peeping through the sky dome tomorrow we'll be on our way. Be sure your fighting and medical gear is in top shape. Thirty of us, including my Creek and Cherokee fighters, will leave from Skidaway Narrows on a sloop for Frederica. Captain Lafitte and the rest of his regiment are already there."

Mother, sitting in her rocking chair, dropped her knitting needles when N.W. reached out and clasped her hands. He spoke softly, almost in a whisper. "Growing up I never thought of becoming a soldier, much less going into battle." He sighed. "Mother, I don't really have a choice. I'm Noble Wimberly Jones, and that means I don't run away from problems." He squeezed Mother's hands. "That's my legacy from you and Father."

Mother kept her gaze glued on N.W. Her eyes were moist but her voice firm. "You'll make a good soldier. I'm sure of it. Once this war is over you can again return to practicing medicine." Mother pressed a tiny cloth object into his hands. "This embroidered 'W' will remind you of your heritage and my love."

N.W. placed the tiny square in his tunic, close to his heart. He patted his heart. "That's where I'll keep it." He stepped aside so Mother and Father could share their goodbyes.

Before dawn even thought about showing its face N. W. and Father got up, slipped into their uniforms, picked up their knapsacks, and walked to Skidaway Narrows where Mary and Johnny Matthews were waiting to bid them goodbye. They found the Marines busy checking out the sloop and testing the oars. Gradually the sun pushed open the doors of night. In the distance N.W. watched as an alligator, hidden by a crop of cattails, slithered into the water. From a nearby tree a cardinal, showing off his red plumage, filled the air with his ode to morning.

The captain announced, "This sloop is for those making up Captain Laffite's Carolina Regiment and Noble Jones' Creek and Cherokee fighters. As soon as everybody is on board we'll leave."

Mary Musgrove Matthews squirmed her way over near to where N.W. was standing. She squeezed his hands and whispered, "Be careful. We'll miss you."

N.W. returned Mary's squeeze and soon turned to Father. "How long will it take us to get to Frederica?"

Cupping his hand under his chin, Father announced: "We should be there by noon. Once we get to Frederica we'll be about 50 miles from St. Augustine."

They had been underway about an hour when N.W. spotted a bald eagle spreading its gigantic wingspan. It swooped down, snatched up a fish in its great talons, and soared back to its nesting spot. "Holy mackerel!" shouted N.W., punching the cadet standing next to him. "Wouldn't it be great if we could turn him loose on the Spanish?"

The previously silent recruits began talking among themselves. N.W. found it easy to identify with their up-and-down feelings.

"I left my sweetheart in Savannah," said one of the cadets.

"My grandfather and grandmother are feeble," said another cadet. "If someone should attack them, I doubt they'd be able to defend themselves."

Finally a shy soldier stated, "I know this is a cowardly thing to say, but I'm afraid. I don't really want to kill someone, and I sure don't want to be killed."

Patting the soldier on his shoulder, N.W. said, "Don't feel alone. You have plenty of company."

N.W. scanned the horizon as their sloop at last moored alongside a line of vessels at Frederica. As far as his eyes could see there were armed soldiers milling around and talking loudly. N.W. jostled his way forward until he found Father. Playfully punching him in the ribs, N.W. said, "Father, in case we get lost from each other, be careful and stay healthy."

Father grew serious. ". . . And the same to you, my firstborn son." N.W. looked on with pride as Father huddled with his Indian recruits.

Seeing a soldier from his sloop struggling with a keg of ammunition, N.W. offered, "Let me give you a hand. Where're you going?"

The soldier nodded his head toward Captain Lafitte. After N.W. helped haul the keg to its resting place, he joined his troops who were bunched around their captain.

N.W. nudged the soldier next to him. "There's General Oglethorpe and he's coming our way. He walks like a man in a hurry to get a job done." General Oglethorpe stood in front of the fort with his back to the cannon. He cleared his throat, and silence filled the air. Oglethorpe's voice was strong, winsome, and inviting. "Men, I'm ready to strike a final blow against the Spanish. Are you with me?"

N.W., caught up in the excitement, joined in the wild display of affection for Oglethorpe. Soldiers discharged muskets, and the ground quaked under stomping feet as the crowd roared their approval.

Oglethorpe smiled, obviously enjoying the adulation of his troops.

Suddenly N.W. tightened his hands into fists and then loosened them. *Oglethorpe's confidence is contagious. I hope it continues once we begin bombarding Castillo de San Marcos.*

Oglethorpe raised his hands and waited for the crowd to get quiet. "Men, it's time we teach the Spanish a lesson they won't ever forget! Get on board with your regiment's leader. We'll travel down the St. John's River until we get to Fort George."

The searing sun of coastal Georgia vented its fury as Oglethorpe's troops sailed toward Fort George. As soon as the first sloop came to a standstill, N.W. watched General Oglethorpe leap onto land. The general was joined by a group of soldiers who began clearing a space for their encampment. Oglethorpe wasted no time handpicking a group of Indians. He told them, "Scout out the land and bring me word of what you see."

It was midnight before the scouts returned. N.W. had yet to fall asleep. He strained his ears to hear their report. "General," one of them said, "we found a Spanish fort. It's located about 20 miles from St. Augustine. If we surprise the garrison, we'll be able to seize their fort."

At daybreak N.W. joined with the rest of his unit in marching toward the Spanish fort. For 16 miles they marched. Wiping away the sweat from his brow, N.W. whispered to the cadet next to him. "How much longer do you think we'll have to march?"

The cadet groaned. "I hope we'll soon be to where we're going! I don't know about you, but this heat is getting to me. Where does the general get his energy? Doesn't he ever get tired?"

N.W. grinned. "Oglethorpe's energy is only matched by his self-confidence. Don't forget that his temper has also been known to erupt when things go sour."

With his next step the cadet's feet became entangled in the snarled roots of a palmetto bush, sending him hurling to the ground. N.W. helped him to his feet. He quickly assessed the cadet's scraped knees and pulled a piece of bark from his pack. He handed it to the cadet, saying, "Chew on this. It will lessen your pain."

The soldiers all expelled a sigh of relief when Oglethorpe said, "At ease, men. We're camping here while I set up plans to take the fort."

N.W. eyed one of the rangers, astraddle his horse, slowly slumping over. "Quick!" shouted N.W. "Calm the ranger's horse while I help the ranger." Meanwhile, N.W. eased the ranger to the ground and jerked open his haversack to find a rag. After dousing the cloth with water from his canteen, he applied it to the ranger's forehead. When the ranger stirred, N.W. gave him the remaining water from his canteen.

Two days later N.W. watched from their base as Oglethorpe's sentries surrounded the fort. Finally the garrison of 50 soldiers surrendered and turned over their nine swivel guns. General Oglethorpe later told his soldiers, "This is a great victory. But before we deploy our battery on St. Anastasia Island we need to capture Fort Mose."

N.W. heard someone ask, "Is that the fort where slaves from Carolina have fled?"

"Yes," answered Oglethorpe. The Spanish promised them they'd be free men if they aligned themselves with Spain." He shook his head. "It's such a pity that a lot of our people are demanding slaves. Slavery is something I'll never agree to!"

Soon Oglethorpe handpicked some Scots and Indians to take the fort. N.W. watched from afar as the Scots, dressed in their kilts and swinging their dirks and broadswords, pounced upon the unsuspecting enemy. Likewise the Indian fighters, wielding their tomahawks, added to the carnage. In short order Fort Mose belonged to the English.

N.W. saw a former slave who had fought for the Spanish writhing in pain, his side split open. When no one was looking he slipped an opium tablet into the man's outstretched hands.

Despite their victory, N.W. was shaken. *Everything seems to be going our way. We've been on the road less than four days and we've gained access to two Spanish forts. Still I get an eerie feeling. This seems almost too easy to be true. What will tomorrow bring?*

Tramp! Tramp! Tramp! N.W. fell into line with the other soldiers as they marched to Matanzas Inlet.

Time passed and N.W. left and joined the other cadets who were putting up their tents.

N.W. gritted his teeth and stomped his feet. "These swamps are filled with malaria-carrying mosquitoes. I wish someone had asked me about a good campsite."

He complained to the officer in charge. "Sir, I hate to bother you, but we're under orders to set up our tents near a stagnant body of water."

The officer growled, "Who put you in charge? Haven't you noticed we're surrounded by water?"

N.W. stood his ground. "I'm one of General Oglethorpe's medical assistants. Mosquitoes that cause malaria breed in stagnated waters. If we don't want most of our army sick, I suggest we camp elsewhere."

The officer sneered and said, "Mr. Medical Assistant, if you don't mind, I'm in charge here—not you."

Drawing himself up to his full height, N.W. countered, "Have it your way, sir. As you say, you're in charge—not me." Underneath his breath N.W. mumbled, *Wait until a large number of our soldiers get sick. You'll wish you'd listened to me.*

N.W. returned to the chosen campsite and began looking for a good spot to set up camp. In a couple of nights, as N.W. was getting ready to retire, a soldier approached him doubled over in pain. "Pardon me," said the soldier. "Someone told me you might be able to help me."

"Yes, I'll be glad to help you. Try to make yourself comfortable while I get you some medicine." The soldier did an about-face and began running toward the woods. "I'll be back!" he yelled. "Lately I spend all my time running to the bushes." When he returned, N.W. gave him an opium pill and placed a wet cloth on his forehead. "Whatever you do," said N.W., "don't drink any of this water!"

N.W. glanced up and his eyes met four other recruits with the same symptoms. N.W. bit his lower lip. *I knew this was going to happen! No one is going to listen to a cadet who dreams of someday becoming a doctor. I wonder if my dream will ever come true.*

Three weeks elapsed before N.W. and Father's paths crossed. "Hello, Father," said N.W. "It's so good to see you! How have you been?"

"I'm working hard trying to convince Toonahowie and his friends that this is really a battle. How about you?"

"I'm fine, but guess what? I have a few questions for you."

Father laughed. "Ask away, son. What's bothering you?"

N.W. grew quiet. He glued his eyes on Father. "What are we waiting on? Why don't we bombard the city?" He shrugged his shoulders. "We march and march, we hurl our cannons at the Castillo and they bounce back, hardly making a dent in its structure. Our naval ships are in the harbor and have forced the citizens of St. Augustine to seek refuge in the Castillo." He moaned. "But still we only switch our positions and march, march, march."

Father ran his fingers around the rim of his collar and rolled his eyes. "Why don't you go talk with Oglethorpe? Perhaps he'll tell you why he's waiting."

N.W. sighed, knowing Father was right. As he reluctantly approached Oglethorpe's campsite under a thatched palmetto, he heard angry voices.

A group of disgruntled soldiers were shouting. "We're going home!" said one of them. Another soldier spat on the ground, saying, "This is like watching a sinking ship!'"

When the soldiers moved on, N.W. poked his head into Oglethorpe's quarters and tapped him on his shoulder. "General," he said, "you're our leader. If you lose, we all lose. Please don't give up on us."

Oglethorpe slumped onto his makeshift bed. He groped for words. "I guess all this griping is getting to me."

N.W. placed his hand to the general's head and jerked his hand free. He stepped back, trying to control his trembling hands. His mind became filled with dreadful thoughts. *I have gotten myself into one grand mess. Why did I ever agree to be Oglethorpe's medical advisor? What if his fever continues to rage? What if he dies?*

In a few minutes N.W. snapped out of his disturbing thoughts. "Sir," asked N.W., "how long have you had a fever?"

Oglethorpe seemed bothered by his question. "I'm not really sure. Since I met with the Indians at Coweta I've had several bouts with fevers." Oglethorpe frowned. "Surely you don't expect me to let a fever stop me from winning this battle?"

N.W. squared his shoulders and looked straight at Oglethorpe. "A fever means something isn't right in your body." He hesitated and then added, "I don't mean to frighten you, but high fevers have been known to kill people."

Oglethorpe bristled. "Young man, are you insinuating I'm about to die?"

N.W. grinned. "No, sir. I suspect it would take more than a fever to slow you down. What I am saying is, I can't keep you healthy if you don't level with me. I have medicine I can give you that will lower your fever."

Oglethorpe mumbled something incoherent and said, "Give me that pill and do what you must!"

N.W. gave the general an opium tablet and kept the general's head cool with wet towels. Even during the night hours N.W. put on fresh damp towels and whispered words of encouragement to Oglethorpe. After a few days the general's fever subsided. Despite Oglethorpe's improved health, he issued no official bombardment of the Castillo.

N.W. was near Oglethorpe's tent one morning when the naval commodore from the British Royal Navy arrived. He saluted Oglethorpe, saying, "A hurricane is heading this way and, as I've been telling you, London has ordered that our blockade against St. Augustine be lifted." He shook his head. "That means we can no longer keep the people from St. Augustine from receiving food and ammunition from the supply boats coming from Cuba."

Oglethorpe stood stiff as a ramrod as he responded, "Thank you for the hurricane warning." With scorn visible in his voice he added, "Lifting the blockade will weaken our cause and enable our enemies to get food and supplies. Please relay my dismay to the proper authorities." The naval officer gave General Oglethorpe a snappy salute and left.

N.W. said, "Sir, I don't blame you for being angry. If you ask me, I think they're afraid to go up against the Spanish."

Oglethorpe grinned. "I didn't ask your opinion, but you're probably right."

Two days later the struggling troops were besieged by a violent windstorm followed by torrential rains. When the waters began slowly ebbing, N.W. sighed and commented, "At least I still have my knapsack and Oglethorpe and I have fresh water." He frowned. "However, the number of water-soaked soldiers who will become sick will greatly rise, and my supplies are running low."

N.W. spotted a burly soldier rushing toward Oglethorpe's makeshift quarters. He was gasping for breath and holding his hand across his heart. "General, General!" he shouted. "At dawn this morning a group of slave soldiers from St. Augustine made a surprise attack on Fort Mose. The enemy was victorious, and many of our finest soldiers are dead!"

N.W. reached out to Oglethorpe, whose face turned ghostly white with tears trickling down his cheeks. Haltingly, Oglethorpe said, "Even I know when I'm beaten. My own men have turned against me, the Navy has lifted the embargo, we've endured a violent rainstorm, and now our enemy has retaken Fort Mose! All I can do is to order our men to retreat."

"But, General," exclaimed N.W. in a loud voice, "you can't leave yet. The Castillo de San Marcos still belongs to Spain! Let's go to Fort Mose and find out what really happened."

"Yes," said Oglethorpe, "maybe it isn't as bad as it sounds."

When they reached Fort Mose, N.W. grabbed his nose and weaved back and forth. *Oh my Lord, it's worse than I expected!* Everywhere he turned he saw decaying bodies covered with flies and other vermin.

He watched as Oglethorpe, who had scoffed at personal danger, trembled. "I've lost some of my bravest fighters," said the general. "N.W., let's go back to my campsite. This battle is over and I've lost it."

Back at his makeshift quarters N.W. looked on as Oglethorpe began writing furiously. When he finished he turned to N.W. "Find your father and tell him to spread this message to our leaders. We must begin retreating from St. Augustine. Meanwhile, I'm going to try one more time to get our naval forces to leave a group of 50 sailors to man our artillery posts until the hurricane season is over."

"Sir," inquired N.W., "what will you do if the naval officers turn you down?"

Oglethorpe threw his hands into the air. "If they refuse my request, then we'll have no choice but to retreat to Fort Frederica."

"Before I deliver your message," said N.W., "I want to remind you of how much you planned on winning this battle and that lots of people you counted on have let you down. Try not to forget the exciting victories you've had." N.W. paused and his face turned crimson. "Your plan could have worked if others had done their part."

Oglethorpe grinned. "That's kind of you. Be quick and deliver my message."

N.W. delivered General Oglethorpe's orders to Father, saying, "We'll be lucky if Oglethorpe makes it back to Frederica."

"Has his fever returned?" asked Father.

N.W. shook his head. "It's worse than a fever. The spark of light in his inquiring eyes has disappeared; the spring in his walk is missing. Father, I think his heart has been broken." Now, tears were streaming from N.W.'s eyes. He asked softly, "How do I go about mending a broken heart?"

Father shook his head and glanced toward the ground. "I'll deliver Oglethorpe's orders," said Father, "and join you at Point Quartell."

When N.W. returned to his campsite some of his fellow cadets cornered him.

"You look worried, N.W. Is it true we were beaten at Fort Mose?"

N.W. grimly shook his head. "Yes, we were badly beaten. General Oglethorpe feels defeated." N.W. hesitated, rubbing his hands together. "For me this means once again having to delay my plans to become a doctor. If we retreat to Frederica, we'll spend the rest of our days wondering when the Spanish are going to come after us." He then mustered a faint grin, saying, "Get ready to march to Point Quartell. The general has called for a meeting with Commodore Pearce."

Upon their arrival at Point Quartell, N.W. listened in as one by one the naval commanders rejected Oglethorpe's pleas.

"I'm sorry," said Commodore Pearse, "but we can't run the risk of attacking the Spanish half galleys. The water at Point Quartell is too shallow. Our big English ships would become sitting ducks for their smaller vessels."

As Oglethorpe and Commander Pearce locked horns, N.W. witnessed a short-lived miracle. The older version of Oglethorpe, full of vim and reckless daring, returned. He swirled around and lined up his troops. With his drummers drumming and his ensigns waving their flags, he defiantly marched his men toward the Castillo de San Marcos. Once again Oglethorpe demanded Spanish Governor Don Manuel de Montiano to bring his troops out in the open to fight.

N.W. got caught up in the general's great display of courage. He mused, *If only he had done this before the massacre at Fort Mose.*

Alas, the Spanish governor turned a deaf ear to Oglethorpe's empty threats, and a dejected General Oglethorpe and his army turned and marched his troops back to Fort Diego.

After two days at Fort Diego, Oglethorpe with the help of his commanders marched the troops to their camp on the southern bank of the St. John's River.

N.W. stood nearby and watched the man who had long been his father's friend lose control of his army.

"You can have your battle plans!" shouted a war-weary soldier. "As for me, I'm going home!"

N.W. took note of the rising anger among Oglethorpe's troops. Soon eight men, including a sergeant and a corporal, deserted. Many who remained began arguing among themselves as to what went wrong. Most of their blame fell on General Oglethorpe.

N.W. sidled up to Oglethorpe and whispered, "Why don't you tell them how the naval officers let you down and how some of your key commanders refused to carry out your orders?"

Oglethorpe shook his head. "Can't you see? They no longer trust me. They're not going to believe anything I tell them."

From that point forward N.W. watched General Oglethorpe withdraw and became a listless bystander. On July 28 the defeated troops—sick, hungry, and greatly disillusioned—straggled their way back to Frederica. It had taken them 24 days to return.

"Father," said N.W., "I need to stay here with General Oglethorpe. Please get word to Mother and Mary Matthews that I'm alright and when I think it's safe to leave General Oglethorpe I'll be home."

"I'll get word both to Mother and Mary," said Father. "However, I'm also staying here at Frederica until Oglethorpe is better."

It was another two months before Oglethorpe would leave his house or engage with others, and for the entire two months N.W. and Father stayed at Frederica.

One day N.W. listened in as Father and Oglethorpe exchanged spirited words.

"Noble, I've made up my mind and you can't change it! I need you at Savannah and that's final!"

Father squinted his eyes and shot back, "Sir, you need me here. You and I both know this will be the first fort the Spanish will invade."

Oglethorpe laughed. "Well, we could cut you in half and let you serve in both places. Seriously, Noble, I can't do what needs to be done at Frederica knowing Savannah is vulnerable to an enemy attack. The truth of the matter is, I know of nobody more capable of defending Savannah's coastal waters than you."

Father reached for Oglethorpe's extended hand. "I'll go, but promise me you'll keep the channels of communications open between us."

As N.W. made his last-minute preparations to return home, he remarked, "We haven't heard the last from the Spanish." He dropped his eyes downward. "The only thing we don't know is when and where they'll strike."

CHAPTER 4

Going Home

N.W. kept his eyes on the mumbling veterans sloshing their way through the muddy waters of the Frederica River. The soldiers scrambled aboard the waiting scout boat and began searching for a settling-in spot.

Following behind them were four scraggly Scotsmen dressed in their tartan kilts and matching high-top socks. Having managed to escape from the ill-fated attack on Fort Mosa, they were now on their way to New Inverness, not far from Frederica.

N.W. listened as General Oglethorpe tipped his hat and addressed the group.

"Brave soldiers, your scout boat, *Georgia,* is equipped with ten oars and three swivel guns. Captain William Germain will lead you home by the backwaters so as to avoid meeting up with any Spanish soldiers."

Oglethorpe placed an arm on Noble's shoulder. "Lieutenant Noble Jones is in charge of getting your paychecks from Charleston. You'll need to stay at Savannah while he takes care of this matter. He's a very busy man, so be patient."

Smiling broadly, Oglethorpe added, "You're fortunate to have among your crew his son, N.W. Jones. He's a great person to have around should you fall ill."

Oglethorpe's face grew somber. "Men, thank you for your service and I'm sorry we didn't win." He bowed his head, turned away, and never looked back at the departing party.

The grumbling soldiers began griping before they'd gone a mile.

"Pray tell me why we can't stop at Charleston and get our checks?" asked a soldier with a stubborn beard.

N.W. listened as his Father replied, "The general gives the orders, and it's our responsibility to obey."

N.W. joined in. "Wouldn't you say getting a late paycheck is better than getting no paycheck?"

Some of the soldiers clapped their hands in appreciation of N.W.'s comments.

However, the elder soldier with the stubborn beard and inflamed with anger shouted, "Master Jones, why don't you shut up? We'd have been on our way home a month ago if you hadn't stayed at Frederica to look after our former commander."

N.W. glared at the soldier who was twice his age and three times his size. "Do you have a problem with me taking care of my sick patient?"

The soldier spat on the ground. "Heck yeah, I do. Your mighty general told us we were going to storm the Castillo de San Marcos and that the Spanish would lay down their arms and surrender. Instead, we marched up and down Anastasia Island daring the Spanish to come out and fight."

"Yeah," said another soldier. "While we marched and marched, Spain's former slaves recaptured Fort Mosa."

N.W. spoke quietly. "I understand why you're disappointed. So am I. As a matter of fact, so is General Oglethorpe. I got him over his malaria attacks, but it's been hard convincing him he's still a great leader. He wasn't killed at Fort Mosa, like some of your friends." N.W. waited a few seconds before adding, "Nevertheless the general has been severely wounded."

The soldier's anger rose. "What do you mean he's been wounded?"

"The general feels it was all his fault that we weren't able to storm the Castillo de San Marcos," said N.W. "His battle scars are in his heart. Most of all his pride has been wounded."

"Don't expect me to feel sorry for him," said the bearded soldier. "It was his fault we lost. He ought to feel guilty. I, for one, hope he trots back to England."

N.W. threw up his hands in exasperation and retreated to the vacant seat by Father. He reached into his knapsack and retrieved one of the articles Doctor Nunis had sent him.

Three hours later the scout boat docked at New Inverness, home of the Scottish Highlanders. As the four Scottish Highlanders moved toward the front of the boat, N.W. asked, "Can I see you to your barracks?"

"Thank you, laddie," said one of soldiers. "You're mighty kind." He leaned his head to one side, rubbing his hands across his chin. "I'm glad to get home, but I'm dreading having to tell so many of our women their husbands won't be coming home."

N.W. kept his eyes peeled on the four Scots as they made their way from the scout boat to the crowd of people waiting with outstretched hands. As the oarsmen resumed their work, N.W. heard in the background the dreadful sounds of crying. Shaking his head slowly, he mused, *War leaves behind fathers who will never return home and mothers and children who must struggle to stay alive.*

The following day it seemed to N.W. that all of the returning soldiers were lining up for and against James Oglethorpe.

For the longest while N.W. said nothing. Instead he spent his time trying to sort out his own feelings. His curiosity got the best of him, and soon he began listening to their comments.

"Neither Oglethorpe nor the trustees are willing to listen to our complaints," said a soldier who previously had been quiet. "The way we distribute our land makes no sense. Why can't I leave my land to my wife?"

Another soldier joined in. "How about me? I only have daughters."

Sarcastically one of them added, "One of these days, with or without Oglethorpe's approval, we'll be able to drink rum in Georgia."

Still another soldier said, "There's another thing I don't understand. How is it that Carolina can have slaves but we can't? Without slaves to till our fields, the colony can never grow."

The soldier who had spoken out so strongly against General Oglethorpe tapped N.W. on the shoulder. "Hey, Sonny. You've been mighty quiet. How do you feel about our complaints? Are you with us or against us?"

N.W.'s face turned red, and he nervously scratched under his collar. "Frankly, I approve of your suggestions. What I don't like is the way you go about trying to get the trustees to change their minds."

"And what would you suggest?"

"Letting the trustees know how you feel is one thing," said N.W. "What bothers me is the way you smear the characters of innocent men who don't openly stand with you. And it doesn't seem fair to me that you blame everything bad that happens on James Oglethorpe."

Having shared his thoughts, N.W. ambled over to his father. ". . . Looks like we've swapped a physical war with one of words. No wonder the general feels so despondent. I'm finding it hard to control my tongue."

By the time they got to Skidaway Narrows, N.W. observed that the entire crowd was on edge with each other and more than ready to get home.

As soon as the scout boat landed, N.W. leaped off and started running toward Wormsloe. As soon as he got home he rattled on the gate, hollering, "Hello! It's N.W. Is anybody home?"

N.W. chuckled as he watched Mary and Mother sideswipe each other in their rush to greet him. Mother beat Mary to the draw and hugged N.W. long and hard. "Where's you father?" she asked.

"He'll be along soon. Father has to see that all of the returning soldiers are accounted for before he can leave."

Mother pulled him aside. "Let me look at you. Hm-m, you're taller and a mite thinner." She chuckled. "But we'll keep you! For the last six months we've lived for this day."

Mary broke into the conversation. "They told us you got back to Frederica in late August," she said. "It's now December. Why did it take you so long to get home?"

N.W. tossed his head to one side. "Neither Father nor I felt it was safe to leave General Oglethorpe. He's humiliated over having to retreat from St. Augustine. He can't stand to hear the terrible things his men are saying about him."

Mother said, "You look like you could use a bath. Mary, draw up several buckets of water while I put up a wooden tub by the hearth."

Dusk was rapidly wrapping itself around Wormsloe when Father arrived. Mother, Mary, and Inigo smothered him with kisses. Father sighed. "Just when I thought I'd squared everything away, Mr. Stephens appeared with a special order from Oglethorpe."

N.W, still soaking his weary feet, took a sip of coffee, and inquired, "Father, what job does he have for you to do this time?"

"Come morning," said Father, "I'll begin searching for a scout boat. Oglethorpe is making me captain of the waterways between Savannah, Charleston, and Frederica."

Inigo spoke up. "N.W., get Mary to tell you about how she chased off an unwelcome Indian."

All eyes turned toward Mary. "One morning," she said, "I peeped through one of our bastions and saw a Creek brave staring back at me. 'Let me in!' he demanded. I primed my gun and pointed it toward his head. I told him, 'If you take one more step toward entering our house, you'll be one dead Indian.'"

N.W. slapped his hands across his thighs. "Did he take another step?"

Mary shook her head vigorously. "No. He turned around and skedaddled through the bushes."

The following morning N.W. lingered in his room, sipping coffee and reading some old medical articles. As he got up to get more coffee, he saw a friend who had served with him at St. Augustine standing in his doorway.

"Excuse me," said the soldier. "I was wondering if you might do me a favor."

N.W. smiled. "What might that be?"

"It's my wife. She's with child and we both agreed we'd like you to be the baby's godfather. Will you?"

N.W. leaned forward. "You don't expect me to birth the baby, do you? The only living creature I've ever birthed was some piglets when I was 10."

The young soldier grinned. "Both of us believe you can do it. My mother-in-law will be on hand to assist you. Please say yes."

N.W. stroked his chin and said nothing. Finally he asked, "Can you tell me when the baby is due?"

"It's due sometime this month. I'm just glad I got home before it happened. My wife was so impressed when I told her how you looked after General Oglethorpe."

"I'll do it," said N.W. "I'll have Father give me a quick lesson on childbirthing. He should be back by tomorrow."

The young father-to-be left, seeming to float on air. N.W. went in search of Mother. "Did you hear that young soldier? He's signed me up to give birth to his firstborn child."

Mother patted N.W. on the arm. "Your father is an expert in birthing babies. He'll tell you exactly what to do. Your main job will be cutting the umbilical cord and being sure the severed place is cleaned and sewed up properly."

In less than a week the young soldier returned wringing his hands. "My wife is in labor. Grab your medicine bag and follow me."

N.W. took the soldier by the hand. "Try to stay calm. Father is also coming. Wait until we saddle up and we'll join you."

With Father prompting the main things for N.W. to do, the birthing went well. N.W. wiped the perspiration from his forehead and glanced over at the new father, who was white as a sheet. N.W. grinned and said said, "The mother and baby are doing well—and I hope you'll survive."

N.W. turned and embraced Father. Stepping back he said, "Father, you and I make a great team. Wouldn't it be great . . . ?" N.W. stopped short from finishing his thought. Instead he said, "Forgive me. For a moment I forgot that tomorrow may spell disaster for us all."

"I understand your feelings," said Father, "and I look forward to one day sharing my limited knowledge of medicine with you. However, until our war with Spain is settled, that will be impossible. You'd be interested to know that I leave tomorrow for Charleston to get the money owed to our soldiers. I won't come home without it."

N.W. laughed. "You'd better not return without it. I'm tired of hearing them gripe."

Father had been gone almost a month to Charleston when N.W. strode up the walkway to Mrs. Penrose's inn. He entered the long room and immediately filled his tankard with coffee and then joined some of his friends at a small table for four. Among them was the young father of the baby N.W. had recently delivered.

"I'm glad to see you're doing all right," teased N.W. "How's my godchild?"

The soldier beamed. "Your godchild, who we named James, now weighs seven pounds and is more than 22 inches long."

Suddenly there was a loud ruckus coming from the entrance to the inn. N.W. turned to see who it was. He recognized several of the men as having been on the scout boat that brought him back to Skidaway Narrows.

"Oh, oh. Look out," whispered N.W. "I smell trouble approaching."

The soldiers wobbled over to the bar. "A tankard of rum for me and each of my cronies," said the soldier with the heavy beard.

Mrs. Penrose, in her homespun navy woolen dress and white apron, eyed the disheveled soldiers and shook her head in disdain. She filled their tankards and said, "Remember, I won't tolerate any roughhousing."

The soldier paid her no mind and whirled around to see who else was in the main room of the inn. He punched one of his buddies in the ribs and pointed toward N.W.'s table. "It's that Jones fellow. You know, the one who Oglethorpe thinks is a dandy."

Another fellow said, "Ask him when we're going to get our checks."

The bearded fellow, carrying his tankard of rum in one hand, weaved his way toward N.W.'s table. As he pulled up a chair and situated himself in N.W.'s face, some of his rum sloshed onto N.W's trim uniform.

There was a moment of deafening silence as N.W. wiped away the spilled rum from his uniform.

The soldier with the foul-smelling breath was inches away from N.W.'s face. "A man goes to war risking his life and what does he get? Is it too much to ask that we get our pay?"

"Father has gone to Charleston to get your checks," said N.W. "He should be back soon."

"Your old man has been in Charleston for more than a month. You don't suppose he got our money and left the country, do you?"

N.W.'s face turned crimson. "Are you saying my father can't be trusted?" Not waiting for an answer, N.W. hopped up and balled his right fist and slammed it against his opened left hand.

The bearded soldier grabbed N.W.'s collar and blurted, "I haven't got any faith in your general or your father. They're both scum to me."

N.W. pounced on the soldier, and in no time the drunken soldier lay sprawled out on the floor with his lip bleeding profusely. Mrs. Penrose rushed in before they had a chance to choose sides and enlarge the fight scene. She jerked the soldier up and told him, "Get your friends and leave my inn immediately or I'll have you put in stocks."

Cursing loudly, the troublemakers exited the inn.

With a twinkle in her eyes Mrs. Penrose turned to face N.W. She threw both her hands against her cheeks. "I don't know what to say. This is so out of character for our up-and-coming young medical doctor."

N.W. blushed. "But Mrs. P.," he protested, "he kept bad-mouthing Father." N.W. shrugged his shoulders. "I know Father takes on way too many jobs, but he hasn't a dishonest bone in his body."

"What you say," said Mrs. Penrose, "is true. However, I think your father would be upset with you letting that ruffian get the best of you. Let's keep this little episode to ourselves. Can I pour you another tankard of coffee?"

N.W. reached out and squeezed her hand. "Thanks for understanding and yes, I could use another cup of coffee."

He returned to his seat and one his friends said, "I was about to ask you if your father had any news about the Spanish."

N.W. grew solemn. "I seldom see Father. He's spending a lot of time getting his scout boat outfitted with a swivel gun and ammunition. He's convinced the Spanish will attack us."

Another friend chimed in, "This waiting game is hard to live with."

N.W. commented, "I'm thinking the Spanish are busy building up their forces, and when we least expect it they'll come sailing down the St. John's River to destroy us." He rubbed his hands together and added, "We must at all costs remain ready to do battle with them. The future of our colony and our very lives hang in the balance." N.W. sighed, placing his hands under his chin. "Maybe . . ." His voice grew stronger. "Yes, maybe one of these days this war will be over and we can pick up our broken dreams and begin all over again." He got up to leave, and his friends did likewise.

The following morning, while sipping his coffee, N.W. slapped his hands against his head and said aloud, "I've been home more than two months and still haven't been to see Mary!" He put down the journal he was reading and headed for the door. "Mother," he called, "I'm going to see Mary Matthews. I'll be back soon."

N.W. rushed to Mary's house near her trading post. Mary responded quickly to his arrival. Sitting alone in her darkened living area, she extended her hand and said, "Thank you, N.W., for coming. It's good to see you."

N.W. stammered. "It seems such a short while ago when you and Captain Matthews married and Edward Walking Stick died." N.W. hesitated. "I still expect to see Walking Stick come running to greet me."

Mary dropped her head. "Now all my children are dead, and once again I'm a widow. N.W., what are your thoughts about our fight with the Spanish?"

N.W.'s eyes grew wide with fright. He threw his hands into the air. "We laid siege to St. Augustine and lost. Heaven help us when they come our way. Mary, they have thousands of soldiers!"

As N.W. stood to leave, Mary patted him on his arm and smiled. "Take care of Georgia's future doctor, and don't underestimate the power of James Oglethorpe and his Indian allies."

A few weeks later N.W. came upon Father and a group of veterans. N.W. moved to the background and listened. One by one Father called the name of each veteran. Before he handed out a check, he had each soldier sign off that he'd been paid. When the last soldier had received his pay, N.W. made his presence known.

Smiling broadly he said, "Good morning, Father. I'm glad you're back from Charleston, and I'm sure glad these fellows got their pay. Will you soon be joining us at Wormsloe?"

Father dropped his head. "Not this time, son. I must leave within the hour for Frederica."

N.W. lifted Father's drooping head and looked him straight in the eyes. "Tell me something, Father. We've been waiting almost two years for the Spanish to return. Where are they?"

Father shrugged his shoulders. "You're right. We've given chase to renegade soldiers, rescued the goods aboard a shipwreck, and tried to calm the fears of our people. However, since St. Augustine we haven't come upon a single Spaniard."

N.W. grinned. "It doesn't take much to get any of us worked up these days. Mention the word Spanish, and all of Savannah grows wild with fear."

Father stood erect. His voice was firm. "Even so, we can't let up our guard. We know some day the Spanish will come to invade our land, and when they do they'll bring a mighty army. What we don't know is when they will land."

"Father," said N.W., "please stop by to see Mother before you leave. It would mean so much to her."

Father looked desperate. "I really must leave right away for Frederica." N.W. exchanged a warm embrace with Father as they went their separate ways.

For the rest of 1741 and well into 1742 no Spanish arrived either at Frederica or at Savannah. Still everyone remained tense and uneasy, as if they were living on borrowed time.

In late February N.W. welcomed Father home from Frederica. "Hello, Father. How are you and will you be with us very long?"

"I hope so," said Father. "Today my scout boat is returning to Frederica without me. I've been assigned to another crew. As soon as we get our crops planted at Wormsloe I'll be making sure no Spaniard slips up our coast."

"Does that mean you'll no longer be making trips to Frederica?" asked N.W.

Noble smiled as he ran his hands through his thick black hair. "You know how that goes. If General Oglethorpe commands my presence at Frederica, then to Frederica I'll go."

No one, especially N.W. or Father, was too surprised when Spanish ships appeared off St. Simons Island on June 22, 1742, two years after Oglethorpe had retreated from St. Augustine. Despite his fervent preparations, Oglethorpe's forces were like a group of pygmies up against a giant—or better still, like David up against Goliath. Do miracles ever happen?

CHAPTER 5

The Miracle

Pacing back and forth, N.W. checked his pocket watch. He crossed and uncrossed his feet as the scout boat from Frederica drew near Skidaway Narrows, halfway between Savannah and Wormsloe. When the crew began docking, N.W. yelled to the captain, "Have you any news about the Spanish?"

The grim-faced Marine captain hesitated before answering, "The Spanish—3,000 strong—have taken Fort St. Simons and have more than 50 armed vessels waiting off shore ready to penetrate Frederica."

N.W.'s face turned white and in a shrill voice he asked, "Is Father still alive?"

The Marine drew near and laid his arm on N.W.'s shoulder. "Yes, your father is alive and he asked me to tell you to stay at Savannah." N.W.'s eyes grew large. He shook his head, not believing what he had just heard.

The Marine captain continued, "He's counting on you to calm the people when this news breaks."

N.W. shook his head. "How can I stay here when I'm needed at Frederica?"

The Marine lowered his voice. "I guess we all knew sooner or later this day would come. You know your father. He'll be in the thick of the fight."

N.W.'s thoughts ricocheted between obeying and disobeying Father. "I think I should get on the next scout boat going to Frederica. If we lose Fort Frederica, it will only be a matter of time before Savannah and Charleston will fall."

"You'll have to decide whether you'll obey your father," said the Marine. "I would like to remind you how much trust he has in you."

N.W. threw his hands into the air. "Oh, my, what a mess! Still, Father is counting on me to see our people through this terrible time." N.W. faced the captain. "I'll go with you to Savannah."

When N.W. and the captain arrived at Savannah they found the women and children running through the streets screaming and looking for places to hide. N.W. cornered an old man and asked, "Have you seen any Spanish soldiers?"

"No, but Captain Milledge from Fort Argyle was here a short while ago and told us the enemy had landed at St. Simons." He drew his trembling hands to the sides of his face. "I'm too old to fight. What can we do?"

"Come with me," said N.W. as he pushed his way to the public square. Meanwhile one of the Marines began ringing the city bell. N.W. took a deep breath and squared his shoulders. His voice remained calm and resolute. "Please try to stay calm. We're going to transport you five miles inland to the village of Abercorn. The Spanish won't think to look for you there. Gather up your most-needed belongings and begin forming a line at the boat dock. A couple of scout boats will soon arrive to help us move you out."

N.W. helped the Marines move the frantic settlers away from Savannah. It was past midnight before N.W. got to Wormsloe. Mother, who had already heard from John the dreadful news, was eagerly waiting N.W.'s arrival. N.W. and Mother remained for a moment inside the walled courtyard of Wormsloe before gradually making their way inside.

"Your father," she asked haltingly, "is he still alive?"

"Yes. You don't think he'll be killed, do you?"

Mother reached for N.W.'s hands. "With all my heart I pray Father's life will be spared." She frowned. "You aren't thinking of going to Frederica, are you?"

"I had every intention of going until our Marine captain told me Father had requested that I stay and defend Savannah." N.W. wrinkled his brow. "If only there weren't so many of them and so few of us."

Mother rocked to and fro. "We can't change the forces fighting against us, but we can ask God for a miracle."

N.W. smiled. "A miracle? You mean like Moses crossing the Red Sea on dry land and the mighty Egyptian army being drowned?"

"Something like that," said Mother. "Only a miracle from God can save the colony of Georgia. Do you believe that, N.W.?"

"I'll join you in praying for a miracle to deliver Georgia from the Spanish," said N.W. He grinned sheepishly and said, "While I'm praying I'll also ask for a miracle that will keep alive my dream of becoming a good doctor for our people."

Night silently ebbed away and morning came peeping through the tall pines encircling Wormsloe. The day passed slowly. It was like waiting for a big explosion. As the shadows of evening began crisscrossing the sky, N.W. said, "Although part of me had rather not know, I'd better get to the port for an update."

N.W. trudged toward Skidaway Narrows, dreading every step he took and fearful of what his ears might hear. When the scout boat came into view, N.W. saw the Marine captain frantically clasping his hands in a victory salute.

Within 15 minutes the sloop had docked and the Marine captain leaped to the ground. He picked N.W. up and literally tossed him into the air. "We beat them! We beat them!" he shouted. "Your father and his ranger crew alerted General Oglethorpe that some Spaniards were less than a mile away. Oglethorpe seized the moment, and his men beat them soundly."

N.W., with tears running down his cheeks, jerked loose. "That's great news! Get out of my way. I need to tell Mother."

Panting for breath, N.W. ran nonstop until he arrived home. He burst into the kitchen, grabbed mother's hands, and began dancing a jig. His face glowed with delight.

"Will you slow down and tell me what this is all about? I haven't seen you this happy since before we went to war."

"We won! We won!" shouted N.W. as he began twirling Mother round and round. "Mother, we got your miracle!"

Mother shoved him gently. "Can you tell me what we won?"

N.W. stopped in his tracks and said, "Sit down, Mother. You're going to find this hard to believe." Mother, her eyes rolling, edged her way to the nearest chair.

"I've just come from the Marine station at Skidaway. The captain of the guard told me that Oglethorpe with a small group of Highlanders, Rangers, and Indians defeated the Spanish."

"Does that mean Father is on his way home?"

N.W. threw his hands over his mouth. "I'm not sure when he'll be home. Never mind that. Father is alive! He's alive!"

The homecoming of N.W.'s father was way overdue. It was a month and a half after the Battle of Bloody Marsh before Father showed up at Wormsloe, where he received a hero's welcome.

After smothering him with kisses, Mother pulled back a little and said, "I was beginning to think we'd never see you again. The last time I saw you was January 18. Both of the big battles were fought in July. It's now August 23. What took you so long?"

"Yeah," said N.W. grinning. "We want to hear from you the details about the battle and what you've been doing since."

"Do you mind if I change into something more comfortable and have a bite to eat before I answer your questions?"

They all backed away and said in unison, "Father, forgive our bad manners. Of course we'll wait."

After eating a hearty meal of shepherd's pie and getting into a change of clothes, Father settled into his favorite chair and began his story. "I'm going to get straight to the heart of the battle. Near Fort St. Simons my rangers and I ran into a small detachment of Spanish soldiers marching toward Fort Frederica. Several of us took off running until we reached Oglethorpe, who was drilling some of his Highlander soldiers. Groping for air, I shouted, "'The Spanish are within a mile of Frederica!'"

N.W. wiggled his way to the edge of his chair. "What did Oglethorpe do?"

"He leaped on the first horse he saw and shouted, 'Follow me!'" Father stopped to catch his breath and leaned back in his rocking chair, relishing the suspense he'd created.

Wringing his hands, N.W. said, "You dare not stop now!"

"Catching Captain Sanchez off guard, Oglethorpe spurred his horse toward Sanchez's troops. Two Spaniards threw down their weapons and surrendered to Oglethorpe. You should have seen Toonahowie! A Spaniard shot him in his right shoulder. Then Toonahowie took his pistol in his left hand, took aim, and killed a Spanish officer."

Mother stood up. "I find all this mindboggling."

Father gave her a quick kiss and continued. "It wasn't long before the Spanish resistance fell apart, and those who were still alive began stumbling wildly in the woods."

"Father," asked N.W., "weren't the Spanish at that time within a mile of Fort Frederica?"

"Yes. Fortunately for us they had became very confused and found themselves going around in circles."

"How many casualities did we have?" asked N.W.

"We lost one Highlander from heat exhaustion. The Spanish had 36 men who were either killed, captured, or missing."

"Oglethorpe, expecting General Montiano to send in the remainder of his huge army to decimate Fort Frederica, went to work situating his men in special spots while he went back to Frederica to get more troops. While he was gone we laid up piles of brush and logs to protect us from their gunfire. We hid in the dense wood near the marshes. A steady rain began to fall."

Father got up and poured himself a tankard of wine before resuming his story. "It was around 3 p.m. when the two armies met again. Someone from Spain's Captain Barba's troops noticed the brush and logs on the far side of the marsh. They approached to investigate and were met by a barrage of English bullets. By the time Oglethorpe reached us we had destroyed the Spanish soldiers sent to find us. This time they lost around 300 men."

"It's late," said Mother. "Could we continue this story tomorrow? Father must be tired. Come, Noble. A good night's rest will do you good." Father got up and, with his hand in hers, followed Mother to their bedroom.

The next morning as N.W. sipped his coffee he said, "Father, I hope you know we're extremely proud to be part of your family! When you finish eating let's hear the rest of your story.

Once again Father seated himself in his favorite chair and picked up where he'd left off. "A few days later Oglethorpe, with 500 soldiers, decided to make a night attack on the Spaniards at Fort St. Simons. A French prisoner escaped, and some of our soldiers were ready to chase him down when Oglethorpe stopped them. Instead he took out an ink quill and asked for some paper. He began writing furiously."

"I'm dying to know what the general wrote," said N.W.

"So was I. Afterwards when the dust settled I asked him what he'd written. Oglethorpe gave me that cocky smile of his and said the note he addressed to the Frenchman promised him 300 English pounds if he could convince the Spanish to move their fleet up the Frederica River. Then Oglethorpe released a Spanish prisoner, thrust the note in his hands, and made him promise to never let the Spanish officers see it."

"Did the note work?" asked N.W.

Laughing loudly, Father slapped N.W. on his shoulder and quipped, "What do you think that Spanish soldier did?"

N.W. grinned. "He must have gone straight to the Spanish authorities. The mighty Spanish army soon retreated back to St. Augustine."

N.W. raised his eyebrows. "Father, I still don't understand why you were so late coming home."

Father wiggled and squirmed. "You know how it is with Oglethorpe. At first he found it hard to believe the Spanish would retreat. When it dawned on him he'd won a great victory, he was determined to make the Spanish pay for humiliating him in 1740 at St. Augustine."

N.W. clapped his hands together. "Now I get it. Oglethorpe convinced you to revisit the gates of St. Augustine!"

Father shrugged his shoulders. "Flushed with pride and self-confidence, we spent 10 weeks confronting the Spanish. At the gates of St. Augustine we challenged Montiano's forces to fight us. They refused. With the rise of bad weather we returned in late August to Frederica."

N.W. smiled. "What does Oglethorpe plan to do now?"

"He'll keep planning for a major offense by the Spanish. In the meantime the trustees are demanding he come to London for a court martial hearing."

N.W. took a deep breath. "Father, how about our plans? Shall I begin hunting us a suitable place to begin our practice?"

Father twisted and squirmed as he always did when he'd rather not speak. Finally he said in an unconvincing way, "N.W., begin your search."

CHAPTER 6

Coosaponakeesa

The muggy days of summer faded into the crisp days of November. One morning after breakfast N.W. and Father fell to talking. "Father," said N.W., "I hear Mr. Oglethorpe's enemies are pushing the trustees to abolish our rum and slavery laws."

Father's face turned red. "You heard right. I hope you saw I didn't sign their petition."

N.W. grinned. "I did notice your name was missing. I know you're in favor of many of their complaints. Why didn't you sign their petition?"

Father cleared his throat and leaned forward. "I'm not comfortable signing on with people who spend their days and nights finding fault with others. If you don't sign their petitions, they consider you their enemy. I find that hard to swallow."

N.W. wrinkled his brow. "I hope you aren't too surprised some day if I sign their papers. Too many people have left Georgia to live in Carolina. And if we can't have slaves, we aren't ever going to be able to farm our land." Sensing he'd made his father uncomfortable, N.W. quickly changed the subject.

"By the way," added N.W., "I haven't talked with Mary Musgrove — excuse me, I mean Mary Matthews—since the Yamasee Indians destroyed her trading post at Fort Venture."

Father's eyes sparkled with mischief. "By all means pay Mary a visit and give her my good wishes. Just be sure you don't sign any petitions while you're gone."

N.W. ducked as Father pretended to swat him. Waving goodbye, N.W. scooted toward the trading post. When he got there he spotted Mary sorting out some fur pelts. "Hello, Mary," he called. "How have you been?"

Mary pursed her lips and clasped her hands. "I'm well, thank you. You're looking great, Master Jones. Can I serve you a tankard of rum?"

N.W. held up his hands in protest. "Oh, no thank you. A mug of coffee will suit me well." He smiled. "It seems only yesterday you shared with me the medical secrets of the white oak."

Mary laughed. "Ah, yes, you were 10 then and so eager to learn. How old are you now?"

N.W. stood tall. "I'm 19."

Mary smiled. "Oglethorpe told me how you took care of him during his attempt to take St. Augustine. Now that we've defeated the Spanish are you still planning to open up your own doctor's office?"

N.W.'s face lit up. "That's my dream. I'm waiting on Father to give me a go-ahead signal. He's promised to let me be his apprentice."

Mary tapped her fingers on the counter. "What brings you here today?"

N.W. clasped his hands together. "When I heard that Fort Venture had been demolished I immediately thought of you. I'm so glad you weren't there when it was attacked."

Mary leaned forward. "Losing Fort Venture made me tremble with rage. However, Oglethorpe's men will make those who burned it to the ground pay for their misdeeds." Suddenly Mary's voice became a whisper. "It's the loss of my loved ones that troubles me most."

N.W. riveted his eyes on Mary and spoke softly. "Would you like to talk about your losses?"

Mary nodded and expelled a heavy sigh. "Let me begin by telling you about my childhood. Mother was the sister of old Brim, emperor of the Creek Indians. Mother married a white trader, and we lived in Coweta. When I was born she named me Coosaponakeesa."

"Glory be!" said N.W. "I'm glad you changed your name to Mary. My real name is Noble Wimberly. I got stuck with N.W. because my father and I have the same first name."

Mary continued. "When I was young they called me Coosa. Even today when I visit Coweta the people call me Coosa." Mary dropped her head. "I was only three when mother died."

N.W. gulped. "So that's when you began learning about losing loved ones?"

Mary nodded. "To make matters worse, Father was away trading furs and couldn't come to her funeral."

N.W. waited while Mary took care of several customers. As soon as she returned he asked, "How did you feel about not having your father nearby?"

"Since I was only three I only vaguely remembered Father. My brother Edward, whom I adore, and I began living with Grandmother. Before Mother died she told me that someday Father would come to get Edward and me. Mother trusted Father to take care of us."

N.W. stretched his hands. "So, when did your father come?"

Mary's eyes grew large. "Father waited seven years before he came! I didn't know whether to run to or away from him. Up until then I knew only the ways of the Creek people. N.W., it frightened me to think of leaving Coweta Town and living among the English."

N.W. slapped the side of his head. "I find that interesting. When I was 10 I left England with my family to start the colony of Georgia, and when you were 10 you left your Indian village to learn the ways of the English."

Mary smiled as she considered the similarities in their backgrounds. "While Father insisted I speak English and learn English ways, he always allowed me to express myself as a Creek at home."

"Did the English children in Pomponne make fun of you?"

Mary threw her hands into the air. "Oh, yes, and even my teachers were hard on me. However, I was a quick learner and didn't want to disappoint Father—whom I soon learned to love and trust. When the Yamasee War broke out between the Indian tribes and settlers of Carolina, for our safety Father moved us back to Coweta."

Mary leaned forward and chuckled. "It wasn't long before young Johnny Musgrove came with his trader father to Coweta. For Johnny and me it was love at first sight. We married in 1725 and moved back to Pomponne, South Carolina. Five years later I was the mother of four children."

N.W., his eyes dancing, spoke up. "You and Johnny were known as the Cowpen turtledoves. I enjoyed Mr. Johnny's booming laugh."

Mary had a faraway look in her eyes. "Do you remember bringing Doctor Nunis to see us when Johnny became sick?"

N.W. propped his hands under his chin. "I do remember going to your house. Doctor Nunis was upset because he couldn't help Johnny. That was shortly after Tomochichi and my friend John Milledge returned from England." N.W. nibbled on his fingernails. "It fell my lot to tell John that his mother and little brother died while he was away."

Mary lightly touched N.W.'s right hand. "That must have been a very hard thing for you to do. Since Oglethorpe was still in England when Johnny died, your father stood in for James at his funeral. His words brought me great comfort."

Mary ran her fingers up and down the counter. "I wish you could have known all my children. My firstborn, David, died in my arms from a raging fever before Johnny and I left Coweta." Mary held her hands over her racing heart. "From our home in Charleston we sent our second son John to Coweta to be taught as a future heir of the Creeks." Mary shook her head sadly. "Both John and my Uncle Brim soon died of raging fevers."

N.W. ran his hands through his thick hair. "My mother lost a child before I was born. She says that when a mother's child dies a part of her dies."

Mary choked up. "That's true. There's something ever so special about a mother and her children. When life is dark and gloomy, children can fill your heart with joy."

N.W. rubbed his knuckles. "We've learned a lot about treating raging fevers, but there's so much yet to learn." His face became fixed. "Mary, we must find a way to keep so many children from dying!"

Mary nodded her agreement and continued her story. "When our people stopped having high fevers we sent our Jamie to Coweta to learn how to govern our people. Alas, three months before his father's death Jamie was found in the woods with a bow lodged in his heart."

N.W. stood up, visibly shaken, and then slowly sat back down. He sighed and began counting on his fingers. "In a few short years you had buried your mother, three of your children, and your husband Johnny."

Mary's lower lip trembled as she wiped her eyes. "Edward Walking Stick was the last of my children to die. Although he's now been dead several years, I still miss him. N.W., do you have any idea how much he loved you?"

N.W. shrugged his shoulders and smiled. "Walking Stick and I were good friends. As you know, I've always had a soft spot for children."

Mary's eyes were glowing. "I remember he came home one day clutching a marble. He smiled and told me he'd been playing hide-and-seek and you gave it to him. When I asked him why you'd given him a marble, he shook his head and replied, 'I don't know. He seemed upset that the other children were laughing at my stiff leg.'"

Mary once again excused herself to wait on traders. While she tended to business N.W. went for a brisk walk. Suddenly it dawned on him that the noonday sun had long since faded. He pulled out his pocket watch and then made a beeline back to the trading post.

"Holy mackerel! Mary, I need to get to our parade grounds for drilling. I wouldn't want to find myself behind bars. Can I come back after we have our drill practice?"

Mary gave him a pat on the back as N.W. scooted out the back door. "Be gone and hurry back," she said. "I'll have a pot of coffee waiting for you!"

Several hours later N.W., weary from hours of drilling and shooting his firearms, returned to Mary's trading post. This time all the traders were gone. She poured him a steaming cup of coffee.

N.W. smacked his lips. "This coffee hits the spot."

"Did you pick up any worthwhile news while you were away?"

N.W. removed his outer tunic and rolled up his shirtsleeves. "My only news is that Secretary Stephens is busy sticking his nose into everybody's private business and some bachelor fellow by the name of Bosomworth is claiming to be a great writer."

Mary chuckled. "I met Thomas Bosomworth several years ago when he became President Stephens' Secretary of Indian Affairs. To say the least, we didn't share a mutual attraction. Imagine my shock last year when he told me God had chosen me to become his wife. I squashed that in a hurry. I told him he was out of his mind and if I ever did remarry, it certainly wouldn't be to him!"

N.W. furrowed his brow. "Let's get back to your story. In Coweta you're an Indian princess. Yet you spend a great deal of your time as an interpreter and treaty-maker on behalf of my people. Why do you do this, Mary?"

Mary laughed. "That's what I've been wondering lately." She leaned over and with her deep blue eyes made direct contact with N.W. "My father was an English trader and my first husband, dear Johnny, had a Creek mother and an English trader for a father. I loved and trusted my father and my husband." Mary smiled and said softly, "There's something else you need to know. I'm fascinated with James Oglethorpe. I've never been able to turn down the multitude of requests James has thrust upon me. He's a charmer, isn't he?" Mary quickly changed the subject.

Making eye contact with N.W., she asked, "Did you ever meet my husband, Jacob?"

N.W. lowered his eyes. "Yes, and I hope we're still friends after I tell you of a little incident that happened shortly before his death."

Mary seemed agitated. "Tell me about it."

N.W. swallowed hard. "I was on my way to Wormsloe when one of Mr. Matthew's friends brushed up against me. 'Aren't you the son of Sir Noble Jones, the friend of the mighty Oglethorpe?'" he asked.

"I pushed away from his foul-smelling breath and stood erect. 'Yes,' I answered, 'I'm the son of Noble Jones. My father and James Oglethorpe were friends before we came to Georgia. What's that to you?'"

"The man glared at me. 'It's too bad your father and Oglethorpe are such good friends. We can't wait for Oglethorpe to leave Georgia and return to England. As for your father, he'll pay dearly for not signing our petition.' Then he pushed me aside, saying, 'What do you think of that?'"

Mary giggled. "Oh, oh, I bet that angered you."

N.W. responded, "I balled up my fist, and soon he lay flattened on the ground. Then I brushed my palms and said loudly, 'That's what I think of that!' If it hadn't been for your husband, our confrontation would have been much worse. Your husband told me to get myself home. Then he gathered his cronies, and they went inside a nearby pub."

Mary frowned. "My husband and his friends, especially after they had too much to drink, often became a rowdy bunch. I became weary making excuses for him. However, we did agree on one thing."

N.W. raised his eyebrows. "What's that, Mary?"

Mary frowned. "Despite his personal failings, Jacob was someone the colonists and trustees feared. He was also a brave defender of my land rights." Mary cast her eye downward and expelled a heavy sigh. "To be honest with you, Jacob and I had our personal squabbles."

N.W. cocked his head. "Oh?"

Mary giggled. "Here I go telling the secrets of my heart to someone 20 years my junior." Mary leaned over toward N.W. "Jacob and I had our biggest squabble when I went with Oglethorpe to Coweta Town. In a drunken stupor he barged into my bedroom and screamed that he couldn't believe I was going to traipse off 400 miles with James Oglethorpe to Coweta! 'Woman,' he said, 'What's got into you? Just what do you expect me to do while you're gone?'

"I looked him sternly in the eye and said calmly, 'It's necessary that I go.' He reminded me that I might be killed. I smiled, reaching out to touch his hands and told him that if that happened then my plantation would be his. Finally I asked him to stay sober while I was gone."

N.W. watched Mary's face turn dark. "I've spent 10 years of my life being a friend to the leaders in Georgia, and what have I received in return?" She paused as her words, hard and cold, tumbled out. "I can't tell you the number of times I've been told that if I did a certain favor I'd be repaid. Instead of being paid I've been handed a bag of promises. Even Oglethorpe tells me he's planning to return to England. When he does he'll be leaving with the trustees owing me a lot of back pay."

N.W. froze in his tracks. He didn't know what to say. Like most of the settlers, he'd come to take Mary's support and trust for granted. He trembled. *Could it be that someday Mary will encourage her Creek Indian friends to declare war on Georgia?*

"Mary," N.W. said softly, "Georgia, now, more than ever, needs your help. I shudder to think what it would have been like all these years without you. Oglethorpe's leaving will bring about a lot of hard changes. Please tell me you won't desert us."

Mary's visage softened. "N.W., I haven't forgotten your kindness when my babies died of malaria nor have I forgotten your father's helpfulness when John died."

Mary patted N.W.'s hands. "Please don't be too hard on me if some of the general's charms are wearing thin. My husband is thrilled when James talks of returning to England. Personally I'd miss him greatly."

N.W. leaned back and propped his hand under his chin. "Is it true that you and Oglethorpe, along with a few Indians and Scottish Highlanders, forged a 400-mile path through a wilderness of dense thickets, swarming insects, and lurking Spanish warriors? Is it also true that your group faced starvation, crossed five rivers, and survived several violent rainstorms?"

"Yes, you're correct," nodded Mary.

N.W. chuckled. "Count me in with Jacob. Mary, why did you go to Coweta?"

Mary's eyes were dancing. "There's something about James Oglethorpe that I find irresistible. He was in danger from 7,000 revolting Indians. He needed those 7,000 Indians to defeat the Spanish." She paused and then began again. "I felt it was within my power to bring my people back into the English fold."

N.W. winked. "Mary, are you in love with Oglethorpe?"

Mary cast her eyes toward the floor. "We enjoy being together. However, I suspect James is too hard on himself. If he has strong feelings for me, he keeps it to himself."

"How about you, Mary? How do you feel about James Oglethorpe?"

"Now that Jacob is dead I'm very vulnerable." She let go a heavy sigh. "I've probably been in love with James Oglethorpe for several years. However, I have my doubts he'll ever return my feelings."

N.W. eyed a long line of traders waiting for Mary, so he excused himself and promised to return soon. He carried away a mixed bag of feelings about the conversation he'd been privy to hear. N.W pondered, *Are Mary and Oglethorpe on a collision course?*

⎯⎯•⎯⎯

The ensuing days turned into months, and the passing months ushered in a new year. While the Spanish were no longer a threat, the colonists were up in arms against each other.

Meanwhile, as N.W. and Father searched to find the best place to set up their medical practice, they stopped long enough to reminisce about recent events.

Father clenched his jaw. "Oglethorpe's gone but our problems remain. The malcontents keep bombarding the trustees with requests. Every day I hear of a family booking passage back to England."

Tugging at his collar, N.W. wondered aloud, "Father, have we waited too long? Those who aren't on their way to England are crossing the Savannah River to take up residence in Charleston."

Father let go a belly laugh. "Since the rum law has never been enforced, repealing it hasn't made any difference."

"They can have their rum," said N.W., "but when they start declaring coffee as illegal that's when I'll stage an uprising."

N.W. drew serious. "Now that Oglethorpe is no longer with us, will you be pushing for removing the ban on slavery?'

"While I'm not totally comfortable with buying and selling people, I see it as the only way we can compete with Carolina. So, I'll sign my name requesting that the trustees rescind their law against importing slaves."

Father went for a tankard of wine and returned. He scratched his forehead. "I've been meaning to tell you, I delivered a letter from James to Mary yesterday. Since the two of you have a special friendship, why don't you pay her a visit?"

N.W. chuckled. "I'll do just that."

Upon arriving at the trading post, N.W. found Mary slumped in a corner of the main room. She was staring into space and twisting a diamond ring off and on her ring finger. Crumpled down on the floor beside her was a letter.

N.W. tiptoed to where she was sitting and whispered, "Father said you got a letter from James. I was hoping to find you with a beaming face. Obviously the news wasn't to your liking."

Mary wiped her swollen eyes and stared blankly at N.W. Her speech was blurred. She pointed to the ring on her finger. "Maybe you can help me make sense of this,"

N.W. drew closer and whispered, "Your ring is beautiful."

He leaped backwards as Mary suddenly became rigid as chiseled stone. She screamed, "I hate this ring and I hate James Oglethorpe!" Now she was weeping again. She picked up the crumpled letter.

"Mary, get hold of yourself. What did Oglethorpe tell you before he left for England? Did he give you the ring that's on your finger?"

Mary struggled to compose herself. She sighed. "It was twilight when James stopped by before leaving the next morning for London. He told me he had a lot of hard questions to answer when he returned to London. He bemoaned the fact that the settlers no longer trusted him and that he'd spent most of his personal finances to fight the war against Spain."

Mary began drumming her fingers on the table. "Then he placed in my hands a pouch containing 100 English pounds and reminded me his people could have never set foot on Savannah's soil without my help."

N.W. watched as Mary began violently twisting the diamond ring on her finger. Once again she let go a flood of tears. In a little while she continued talking. "He looked me straight in the eye and told me he'd be back. Then he took this diamond ring from his little finger on his right hand and placed it on my ring finger. He hugged me tightly and asked me to wear his ring as a lasting remembrance of our friendship." She paused and her voice became soft.

"The last thing James did was something he'd never done before. He kissed me. Then seconds afterwards, as if he were trying to mask his real feelings, he turned and left."

Mary's hands trembled as she pointed to the part of the letter that had ripped out her heart. "He's married an English heiress and is never coming back to Georgia!"

N.W. was speechless. He buttoned and unbuttoned his jacket. "I understand why you're hurt. I'm thinking the trustees convinced Oglethorpe that a marriage of convenience was the only way he could salvage his family estate."

Once again Mary became rigid as chiseled stone. "I'm not buying that. James Oglethorpe always makes up his own mind. He's deserted the colony and crushed my heart."

Mary rose to her feet and flung Oglethorpe's ring to the floor. "I'll fight fire with fire. Nobody is going to ignore Coosa, Empress of the Creek nation!"

N.W. slinked out the back door, trembling with excitement. *Will Mary get over being spurned, or will she turn her Creek Indians against Georgia? One thing is certain: Father and I won't be opening our practice anytime soon.*

CHAPTER 7

Mary's Revenge

When N.W. arrived home he was breathless and his eyes were bulging. He tugged on Father's arm. "Father, sit down. I've just come from the trading post, and Mary is madder than 10 angry bobcats."

Father rubbed the back of his neck. "Does this have anything to do with the letter she got from Oglethorpe?"

N.W. nodded. "It has everything to do with that letter. Did you know that before Oglethorpe left for England he gave Mary a diamond ring?"

Father raised his eyebrows. "Do you mean the diamond ring he used to wear on his little finger?"

"Yes, that's the ring. Mary also said that Oglethorpe told her that as soon as he cleared his name he'd be coming back to Georgia."

Father said, "Son, I know you take great stock in Mary, but I'm not sure she always tells the truth."

N.W. rolled his eyes. "I only know what I saw. I've never seen Mary so upset. She showed me her letter where Mr. Oglethorpe told her he wasn't coming back to Georgia and that he'd married someone from England. You need to know she's determined to get the land and money due to her."

Father laid his hand on N.W.'s arm. "For now let's keep this between the two of us. Three months from now Mary may feel different about the matter."

N.W. turned his hands upside down. "I'll do as you say, Father. You certainly know women better than I. Changing the subject, what have you heard from John Milledge?"

Father smiled, "Please, show your respect. He's now Commander Milledge in charge of Fort Argyle. I hear he's working to secure ownership rights to a large parcel of land near the fort. Why don't you pay him a visit?"

"That's a jolly good idea. I'll leave first thing in the morning."

The next day N.W. rode his horse at a steady clip through the rough-hewn coastal roads. It was late evening when he arrived at Fort Argyle.

"Halt! Who goes there?" said a sentry.

"I'm N.W. Jones and I'm here to see Commander Milledge."

"Wait here. I'll see if he's disposed to receive you."

It wasn't long before N.W. spotted John swaggering down the road. He quickly tied his horse to a hitching post, leaped off his horse, and ran to meet John. N.W. doffed his hat, saying, "Good evening, commander. You're looking well. Since I missed your recent trip to Savannah I decided to come and check on you."

"My goodness!" exclaimed John. "It's been at least two years since we've had a chance to talk. Come with me. I have someone I want you to meet."

When they arrived at John's house he called out, "Margaret, we have company." Soon a young lady came to meet them. "N.W., I'd like you to meet Margaret, the lady who stole my heart."

N.W. burst out laughing. "So you're the secret Father wouldn't divulge to me. Hello, Margaret. I'm happy to meet you."

"Come inside and make yourself at home," said Margaret. "John speaks so often about you that I feel like I've known you for many years. I believe you prefer coffee to tea."

"Yes," responded N.W. "I'm pleased he remembers."

After washing his hands N.W. sat down and began sipping coffee.

John's eyes were dancing with devilment. "How about you, N.W.? Isn't it time you settled down with a wife and began increasing our number of Georgians?"

N.W. blushed. "Believe me, the notion has occurred to me many times. However, right now I'm in no position to support a wife, much less a brood of children. I'm still waiting on Father to accept me as his apprentice."

John leaned back in his chair and ran his hands behind his neck. "Have you heard the latest love story to hit our colony?"

N.W. leaned forward. "No, but I'm all ears. Who is it this time?"

"This is the way the story came to me," said John. "It seems Mary Musgrove Matthews and Thomas Bosomworth were both passengers on a scout boat coming from Savannah to Frederica."

N.W.'s face turned white, and he leaped to his feet. "I thought Bosomworth was still in England. When did he return to Savannah? Did he and Mary get in a fist fight or cozy up?"

John laughed. "The Reverend Bosomworth has been back from England for several months. The two of them eloped to Darien, and we're all invited to a huge wedding celebration to be held later in Savannah."

Margaret entered the conversation. "N.W., the wedding celebration is bound to include music and dancing. Is it all right with you if I bring along a friend of mine to the occasion?" She touched him softly on his arm. "If my friend doesn't interest you, we'll understand."

N.W. smiled. "Welcome to my matchmaker's club. Margaret, I'd like to meet your friend."

Facing John, N.W. ran his hands through his hair. "I was hoping for a longer visit, but I'm not sure how Father is going to react to this recent love match between Thomas and Mary. I'm thinking he'll need me."

"You can't leave before I show you my cattle and horses," said John. "I have my claim for the land before the trustees, but as of yet I've heard nothing from them."

"I'm not about to leave until I see your land and animals. I remember those terrible days when your father and mother died and Reverend Whitefield snatched Richard and Frances and carted them off to his orphans' home." N.W. placed his arm on John's shoulder. "But, you, John, never let any of those setbacks stop you. You're quite a remarkable man, and I'm proud to call you my friend."

After saying goodbye to Margaret the next morning N.W. and John rode out see the land John had amassed. Sitting astride his saddle, N.W. said, "John, I really like your wife. It does my heart good seeing you happy and so successful. It couldn't happen to a nicer fellow."

John's eyes watered. "Thanks. You and I have been through some troubling times, haven't we? One of these days you're going to be Georgia's premier doctor. Thanks to Doctor Nunis, you're already on your way. By the way, have you heard anything from Doctor Nunis since our war with Spain?"

N.W. dropped his head and said softly, "I thought you knew. Doctor Nunis died in 1744."

"I'm sorry to hear of his passing. At least he lived long enough to know Spain was no longer a threat to Georgia."

"That's true. His son Moses is on his way from New York to Savannah and is bringing me a package his father prepared for me shortly before his death." For a while neither John nor N.W. said anything, hating to say goodbye. Finally N.W. tugged on the reins of his horse. "John, I need to be on my way. I'll be looking for you and Margaret at the Bosomworth party. Say hello to your brothers and sisters for me."

All his way home thoughts of Mary filled N.W.'s mind. *Has she, as Father suggested, forgotten about James Oglethorpe, or did she marry Thomas Bosomworth solely to spite James Oglethorpe?* He shook his head. *I can't erase Mary's angry face when she realized Oglethorpe wasn't coming back to Georgia and had married an English heiress.*

N.W. was relieved when he at last found himself reining in his horse at Wormsloe. He fed and watered his steed and hastened to find Father. "You aren't going to believe what John told me."

"Does it have anything to do with your friend Mary Musgrove Matthews?"

N.W. raised his eyebrows. "How did you know?"

Father grimaced. "Would you believe it? Thomas and Mary began their romantic rendezvous on my scout boat."

N.W. gently slapped his hand across his cheek. "Father, what do you know about Thomas Bosomworth?"

". . . Enough to know that I'm not overly impressed with him. He came to Georgia as President Stephens' secretary, then he switched to being in charge of Indian affairs, and then he declared himself a writer. Now he's back in town as our Anglican minister."

N.W. laughed. "Let's hope he's better than our ministers who came before him. I'm having a hard time picturing Mary as a minister's wife."

Father sighed. "We'll have to wait and see how this turns out. Perhaps our worse fears will evaporate."

"Oh, Father," said N.W. "I forgot to tell you that Doctor Nunis' son is on his way back to Savannah."

Father looked surprised but made no comment.

By now the news of the Bosomworths' wedding feast had buzzed throughout Savannah. The women scrounged around trying to piece together a fitting outfit. Even those who spent their days finding fault ceased griping—at least for a while. N.W. lost no time looking for an opportunity to talk with Mary. He caught her transferring some things from her house to her new residence.

"Hi, Mary. Let me help you."

"Thanks, N.W. I could use an extra hand."

"Mary, I want to offer you my congratulations and to wish the two of you much happiness."

Mary avoided looking at him. As they walked along he whispered in her ear, "Are you okay?"

Mary turned and faced N.W. Her voice sounded strained. "I married Johnny for love. I married Jacob for protection. I've married Thomas for . . ." She twisted her hands in frustration. "Let's put it this way: Thomas and I need and deserve each other."

N.W. took a step backwards. "I don't understand."

Mary chuckled. "N.W., stop worrying about me and think of yourself. Do you have a dancing partner for my big event?"

N.W. nodded his head. "My good friend John Milledge is seeing to that. Supposedly he and his wife Margaret have the perfect doctor's wife waiting to meet me."

The two parted company and didn't see each other again until the day of the wedding feast.

⸺⸺

N.W. caught his breath when he saw Mary in her favorite blue silk dress with her hair pinned at the nape of her neck, highlighting her firm chin and high cheekbones. Standing beside her was Thomas, tall and imposing, dressed in his white linen surplice with its wide flowing sleeves.

After the rambling welcome speeches from the various dignitaries, the people gathered around three long tables not too far from President Stephens' house. The tables groaned with food. Mary moved with ease throughout the crowd, making sure everyone felt welcome. After the people had their fill of food and had drunk more than their share of wine and rum, the dancers moved back inside Stephens' house.

By now John and Margaret had found N.W. and introduced him to Sarah Davis.

"N.W," said Margaret, "I'd like you to meet my good friend Sarah Davis. Sarah, meet N.W. Jones."

"Margaret," whispered N.W., "she's beautiful." Turning to Sarah he bowed and inquired, "Would you do me the honor of being my partner at the dance?"

Sarah took him by the hand. "Lead the way. I'm here to have fun."

The fiddlers were tightening their strings, and soon the house was filled with music. Sarah and N.W. danced until the wee hours of the morning, and in between their dances they talked.

"I normally find it hard to talk with strangers," said N.W. "With you, Sarah, I feel like I've known you for a long time."

Sarah's face glowed. "Thank you for a wonderful evening, but I really must get home. Can you help me find John and Margaret?"

N.W. tugged on her arm. "When can I see you again? You will see me again, won't you?"

Sarah laughed. "Yes, I'll see you again."

When they found John and Margaret, N.W. whispered to John, "Don't be surprised if some day she becomes Mrs. Jones."

⎯⎯•⎯⎯

The ensuing months erupted into profound marital problems for the Bosomworths.

"N.W." said Mary, "we need to talk."

"What's up Mary?"

"It's Thomas and me. He told me my place was by his side and not gallivanting over the countryside. I reminded him I was queen of the Creeks and some of them were about to side with the French. Then he forbade me to go talk with them." She bristled. "That did it! No one forbids Mary. I'm the one to choose whether I go or stay. 'Very well,' Thomas said. 'Don't expect me to be here when you return. I'm going back to England.'"

CHAPTER 8

Mary, Mary, Quite Contrary

It was only a few days before the town gossips were busy spreading the news that Thomas Bosomworth, having stripped the parsonage clean as a hound's tooth, had left Mary and returned to England.

Worried, N.W. left immediately looking for Mary. Not finding her at the parsonage, he went to her trading post where he found her surrounded by a stack of fur pelts. Mary's bright blue eyes were dark and foreboding.

N.W. approached her cautiously. "Hello, Mary. Are you alone?"

Mary shoved a fur pelt to one side. "Oh, yes, I'm alone. That pompous rascal, Thomas, did exactly as he promised. He's gone back to England, and frankly I'm glad. If there's anything I can't stand, it's having someone tell me what I can or cannot do!"

N.W. frowned. "No sooner do we get out of one war until we're threatened with a new one. I hear the French in Louisiana are doing everything they can to turn your Creek Indians against Georgia and Carolina. Mary, we have to have your help."

Mary nodded her head. "That makes you smarter than Mr. Thomas Bosomworth! He's so in love with himself that he could care less what happens to Georgia. N.W., I had to talk with my people so they would remain loyal to the English."

"How did they respond?"

"They listened to my counsel. And if the French should ever attack Georgia or Carolina, we'll have the cooperation of the Creek nation."

N.W. wiped his forehead. "Mary, you did Georgia a big favor. Thank you."

As the weeks and months unfolded, Mary kept busy with her responsibilities at the trading post along with nurturing good Creek and English causes. Meanwhile the residents of the colony were sending reams of letters to the trustees, imploring them for radical changes. An exception resided in N.W. Jones, whose romance with Sarah Davis was getting serious.

After dinner one evening N.W. pulled his chair over to where Father was sitting. "You and Mother seem a perfect match. How did you go about finding her?"

Father chuckled. "It was quite simple. She was available, and I was available. My father had a talk with her father, and we got married." With a devilish grin on his face, Father asked, "What are you really wanting to tell me?"

N.W. blinked. "I've met the woman I want to marry, and I need your help in making sure she doesn't get promised to someone else."

Father smiled. "Who might this lady be that has stolen the heart of my son?"

"Her name is Sarah Davis, and she lives with her family in St. Philip's parish. I met her last year at the wedding party given by Mary and Thomas Bosomworth. John Milledge's wife, Margaret, is responsible for bringing us together."

Father grew serious. "Why do you think Sarah is the one for you?"

N.W. was all smiles. He started counting on his fingers. "She's healthy, intelligent, loves her family, and is a good listener." He paused. "If that isn't enough, she makes me laugh."

Father placed his hand on N.W.'s shoulder. "Tomorrow you and I will make a call on Mr. Davis. I'm certain you know you aren't in any position to marry immediately. Right now you have only your good name and my dowry. Sarah will have to wait until you establish yourself as a credible doctor. Do you think she'll be willing to wait on you?"

N.W. nodded. "I have reason to believe she will. She knows how much I'm committed to becoming a doctor, and she understands my current status."

The following day N.W. and his father rode their horses over to the Davis house and had a heart-to-heart talk with Sarah's father. Sarah's father gave the engagement his resounding approval.

Mr. Davis extended his hand to Father and then turning to N.W. said, "It gives me great pleasure that in the near future my Sarah and you will become husband and wife. All I've heard this past year is N.W. said this, N.W. did this, N.W. thinks . . . Would you like to spend some time with your future wife?"

N.W. winked. "That would please me to no end." After a lengthy visit between N.W. and Sarah, the two lovers said their goodbyes and N.W. and Father returned home.

Savannah was once again buzzing over the news that after a year's absence, Thomas Bosomworth was again returning to Savannah. N.W., fearful of what this news may mean personally to Mary and to the colony, made fast tracks to find Mary.

"Mary, what if Thomas asks you to take him back? Will you agree?"

Mary bristled. "Me take that old fool back? I can't imagine a situation where the two of us would begin again."

A few weeks later when Mary saw N.W. approaching the trading post, she threw her hands in the air laughing. "I know you think I'm crazy, but I'm taking Thomas back."

"What did he do or say that changed your mind?"

"He started off by asking me to forgive him. He said it was selfish of him to think I would neglect my role as peacemaker between my people and the English. He also said he'd had a long time to think things over and realized he'd been unhappy in his role as a priest. 'Mary,' he said, 'Look, I'm no longer wearing my canonical robe. From now on I want to serve as an investor. If you and I unite, nobody can stand in our way.'"

N.W. was at a loss as to what to say. Finally he stammered, "I hope this new alliance meets all your expectations."

Throughout the remaining year N.W. made several attempts to talk with Mary, but she always brushed him aside. N.W. confided to Father: "I'm worried about Mary. She seems irritated when I show up. I can't exactly explain it, but she's totally different since Thomas returned from England."

Father replied, "It's Thomas Bosomworth I'm worried about. As I told you before, I have a very low opinion of him. He can't be trusted!"

Another year came and went with Mary and Thomas thriving in their new trading post, "The Forks." Suddenly, with the force of lightning, the

Bosomworths made a decision that cast gloom over the entire colony and Savannah in particular.

Long after everyone else was asleep N.W., as was his custom, was still reading a medical journal and sipping coffee. Suddenly he heard the shrill sound of Indian war hoops and the steady beats of tom-toms. He reached for his pistol and roused Father. "Wake up. We have Indian visitors down at the old Musgrove trading post."

Father threw on his trousers, and together they began rounding up the Georgia Rangers. Since it was still nighttime they used torches to light their way to the old trading post. As the blackness of night merged into the gray streaks of early morning, N.W. found the field filled with Indians repeatedly firing their guns. He scanned the open field and spied Mary and Thomas Bosomworth in a cloistered cove of trees. N.W. listened as his father, astride his horse, demanded, "Who is in charge here?"

Thomas stepped forward. "Good day, Captain Jones. Mary and I have come to do business with President Stephens." He expanded his hands. "We brought along Chief Malatchi and some of his braves just in case Stephens refuses to listen."

Father's face was grim. "Lay down your arms! You can't advance into our city brandishing your guns." The Indians glanced around and, seeing they were surrounded by armed soldiers, laid down their arms.

When he spied Mary, N.W. threw his hands to his mouth. Her hair was in tight plaits held in place with a beaded red band around her waist. She wore a deerskin dress dyed red. Her face was painted with jagged streaks of lightning crescents on her forehead and circles on her cheeks indicating her kinship with Sister Moon and Brother Sun. Mary held her head regally. Her eyes were fierce and unafraid.

Wow! Mary is here to claim her possessions. This doesn't bode well for our colony.

N.W. rushed over to Father, who was staring down at the Indians from his cavalry horse. "Father, when we get to the courthouse can I move up closer so I can hear what's going on? If trouble erupts, perhaps Mary will listen to me."

Father scowled. "That might be a good idea, but if this affair doesn't end this morning we'll need you to help in patrolling Savannah during the night hours."

President Stephens had been expecting the unwelcome guests. Nevertheless, he stayed inside and sent one of his aides to tell Mary's group they'd have to come back the following day.

N.W. watched as Mary stomped her foot and whirled around. Slowly Mary, Thomas, and Chief Malatchi returned to rejoin the spirited Indians they'd left at their campsite.

Father dismounted, walked over to N.W., and whispered, "Even if they've surrendered their guns, the Indians will probably cause an uproar tonight. Be ready. They're upset by the rumor that Mary is going to be put in chains and shipped to England."

N.W. bristled. "I'd never stand for that! Why doesn't President Stephens meet with them and grant her the three islands? You and I both know that Tomochichi gave them to her several years ago."

Father frowned. "That's true but two of the islands have already been sold!"

"Does Mary know that?" asked N.W.

"No and let's pray she never does. Not only have they been sold, but they also were bought by members of President Stephens' council." Father sighed deeply. "The best Stephens can do is to discredit Mary's claims by making it nigh impossible for her to get a land settlement."

N.W. and Father parted, and N.W. began patrolling the area close to where he and Father planned to open their apprenticeship. At first it was relatively quiet. Then the beat of Indian tom-toms began filling the air. The nervous townspeople stayed locked behind their bolted doors and resorted to peeking out of their tiny window slots.

After his all-night vigil, N.W. gulped down a tankard of coffee, washed his face, and made his way to the courthouse. Mary, Chief Malatchi, and Thomas were already there. Behind them, sitting in little pods, were more than 100 Creek Indians. Finally President Stephens opened the door and greeted Thomas and Chief Malatchi. He nodded toward Mary, telling her she could stay and interpret their deliberations. Mary opened her mouth to speak, but Thomas took over.

"Honorable President and loyal servant of the trustees," said Thomas. "We come in peace to ask you to grant Queen Coosaponeeska title to the lands granted her by Chief Tomochichi before his death and reaffirmed recently by Chief Malatchi."

There was a long pause. Still avoiding contact with Mary, President Stephens said in a sarcastic voice, "Bosomworth, please inform Mary that her land deeds are worthless. We obtained the islands in question through treaties James Oglethorpe made with her people."

From his perch nearby N.W. mused, *President Stephens is totally ignoring Mary. That's a big mistake.*

Mary moved until she was inches away from Stephens. She yelled, "I don't need Thomas to tell me anything. I heard every word you said. Let's get something straight. The Georgia colony doesn't own a foot of this land. It all belongs to the Creek nation! I personally wrote the treaties and know what they say."

President Stephens jerked at his collar. "Are you through?"

"Heck, no!" screamed Mary, pointing her finger in his face. "Knowing how crazy English law is, Thomas and I bought St. Catherine's, Ossabaw, and Sapelo from King Malatchi. We paid him in cloth, gunpowder, bullets, guns, and breeding cattle."

Stephens gritted his teeth. "Thomas, tell Mary that if she has proof of her land purchases she must submit her claim to the trustees in writing and provide them a copy of her purchase papers and evidence from someone who lived in the colony when the original treaties were signed." Stephens sneered at Mary, dusted off his jacket, and left.

In a few minutes he returned. Completely ignoring Mary, he put his arm around Chief Malatchi's shoulder. "Why don't we men folk talk this over as friends. Some good food, a bottle of rum, and some gifts should make us all feel better."

N.W. watched as arm in arm Chief Malatchi, Thomas Bosomworth, and President Stephens strolled toward the president's private quarters. His eyes followed Mary who, struggling to regain her composure, retired to her scrubby room. N.W. followed at a distance and watched as she quenched her anger with a bottle of rum.

N.W. cleared his throat to let Mary know she had a visitor.

Mary looked up, trying to hide her trembling hands. "Where did you come from?"

"I've been hanging around the courthouse for the past three days, trying to make sense of your troublesome visit."

"You don't think I should be here, do you?"

N. W. shook his head. "No, I don't. Mary, you've changed! What happened to the Mary who for more than 10 years brought peace between our colony and her people? You no longer seem to care about anyone except yourself."

Mary wobbled to her feet, swallowed another tankard of rum, and pushed N.W. aside. "Get out of my way! I'm going to find those partying blockheads and tell them a thing or two."

N.W. thought, *Mary is making a complete fool of herself. She's making enemies instead of winning friends. Stupid me! What made me think she'd listen to me?* Then he whirled around and hastened to President Stephens' house, arriving just as Mary barged through the door demanding to be heard.

N.W., with his smattering of Creek words, heard Mary yell in Creek to Chief Malatchi something about chains.

Tall, handsome Chief Malatchi, who obviously had also consumed way too much rum, shook his head in disbelief. Then his eyes darkened, and he jerked away from President Stephens. He shouted in Creek words that an angry Thomas Bosomworth quickly interpreted. "Chief Malatchi says that if you put Mary in chains, we'll untie her. Mary is our queen!"

The party abruptly ended. Stephens and his cohorts scrambled around, trying to avert an uprising. Someone seized N.W.'s arm and said, "Get this woman out of here. Lock her up. I do believe she's gone mad!"

N.W. brandished his gun and said, "Let's leave, Mary. You brought this on yourself. Perhaps when you sober up we can talk."

Mary's eyes flashed with anger. "Talk, talk, talk. That's all you English know to do. I want my money and my land, and I want it now. Take your filthy hands off me!"

Stunned by her bitter remarks, N.W. locked her in her jail room and left.

Mary remained in jail while Thomas continued to demand from President Stephens their title deeds. The Indians, several hundred of them, remained at Mary's old camp site, and the Georgia Rangers, under Capt. Noble Jones' command, patrolled the streets day and night for weeks.

N.W. took advantage of the lull and slipped away to check on Sarah Davis.

As he was tying his horse to the hitching post, Sarah ran to meet him. His lips found hers and they remained embraced, saying nothing for a good while. Sarah stepped back a little and asked, "Aren't the Indians ever going to leave? We hear their eerie tom-toms beating during the night hours. How did you get away?"

N.W. smiled. "I snuck away. I had to find out if you were alright and if you needed anything."

Sarah smiled. "We're fine and our food supplies are adequate. Won't you come inside?"

N.W. refused to let go of her hand. "I'd like that very much, but I'd better hurry back before someone discovers I'm missing. There's one bright note. Father keeps reminding me that as soon as Mary and her friends leave, we'll start our apprenticeship."

Sarah clapped her hands. "I'll pray that they'll soon decide on their own accord to leave peacefully. Isn't Mary the Creek lady you're so fond of?"

N.W. shuffled his feet. "That's all in the past. Now Mary hates me. Give me a kiss and let me leave. I hope to see you again soon."

As N.W. wound his way back home, he came upon John Milledge at the edge of the settlement. He gave John a snappy salute. "Do you have any new developments on our unwelcome guests?"

John was all smiles. "As a matter of fact, I do. We had a meeting earlier today, and Chief Malatchi and his tribesmen have agreed to leave."

"That's the best news I've heard in a long time. How about Mary?"

John laughed. "She's still sulking, but at least she's sober. Thomas talked the magistrates into letting her go free under his custody. Oh, I forgot. She sent word that she wanted to see you."

N.W. caught up with Mary as she was packing to leave. "Mary, John said you asked to see me."

At first Mary dropped her head, refusing to make eye contact with N.W. Finally she said. "I've been told that several weeks ago when you arrested me I lashed out at you." Slowly she raised her head and her eyes made direct contact with N.W. "Can you forgive me?"

"Yes, I forgive you," said N.W. "You were both angry and drunk." He paused and propped his hand under his chin. "Mary, do you remember what Tomochichi told General Oglethorpe when he asked how many troops he should bring with him to Coweta?"

For the first time in months Mary seemed relaxed. "He told him to take no one but himself and to speak softly and honestly with the gathered chiefs."

"Mary, you're never going to make President Stephens listen to you. Your angry words about my people and me have forged a barrier between us that only you can mend. Your best hope, as I see it, is to personally take your claims to the trustees." He paused. "For old times' sake I wish you well."

They parted and N.W. joined Father and his rangers in overseeing the month-long siege evaporate as Mary and her Creek friends retreated from Savannah. Like a rapidly spreading fire the simple words, "They're gone!" spread throughout Savannah. One by one, doors flung open and the people took to the streets.

A couple of weeks after their unwelcome guests had left, N.W. and Father met at their new practice site. N.W. announced, "Before another catastrophe erupts, let's open our apprenticeship!"

Father nodded. "I agree. Here, help me put this post in the dirt." Once the post was firmly grounded, N.W. attached a sign to it that read: **Doctors Noble Jones and Noble W. Jones, Esq**.

In no time an eager crowd converged, lining up to be treated.

CHAPTER 9

Transitions

1748–1756

"It seems as if I'm in the middle of a wonderful dream," said N.W. as he pointed to the new office sign. "Since I was a child I've yearned for this day." Putting his arm on Father's shoulder, N.W. continued, "If I'm dreaming, please don't wake me."

Father ran his hands through his thick mop of hair and smiled. "You aren't dreaming, so how about lending me a hand? Once we've put our medicine and instruments in place, we'll decide on our office rooms and the routine we'll follow."

In a few hours they had their equipment situated, and soon Father began unraveling what he had learned about medicine. "Truth is, my medical learning has been a lot by trial and error. A good doctor from London took me under his wing and shared with me how to birth a baby, how to take care of surface wounds, and the best cures for common ailments. Under Doctor Nunis you've picked up a lot of medical skills I've never been privy to."

"Father, you were a great help when I was called upon to deliver my Army friend's newborn. Why don't I watch and take notes as you deliver infants until I feel certain I can handle that skill on my own?"

Father agreed and for the first six months or so N.W. mainly observed as his father oversaw the delivery of new babies from Savannah to the outer reaches of the colony. N.W., as had been his custom since early childhood, bombarded Father with questions. "Shouldn't you clean your cutting instrument after each birth?"

"That's a pile of nonsense. Where did you come up with that idea?"

N.W. folded his hands under his chin. "You know me, Father. I have my own theory about cleanliness. It seems to me germs have a better chance to grow and do us harm when they're unchecked."

Father looked at N.W. with questioning eyes. "You and your theories. If you don't mind me asking, why are you always keeping such close tabs on the weather?"

"On our way from England to Georgia, Captain Thomas explained to me the effects of the sun and moon on ocean travels and how weather affects so many things. I'm following a hunch that weather and health conditions are connected. Maybe, just maybe, I'll figure out the connection."

Father shook his head, saying nothing.

Every evening after they'd seen their last patient N.W. leaped on his horse to go visit with Sarah Davis.

N.W. was enjoying being a willing pupil of his father for nearly a year when the trustees lifted their embargo on slavery.

"Father, doesn't it bother you that these slaves we'll get have been torn away from their homes?"

Father was quick to answer. "Yes, it bothers me. That's why I fought to have a penalty of death put upon any master who kills one of his slaves. I hope we don't ever become like our Carolina neighbors who are often cruel to their slaves."

Leaning back in his chair, N.W. added, "I'm convinced Georgia won't survive without slave labor. A good slave hand can do the work of 10 white men. Still, I'm uncomfortable with the idea many Carolinians have that Negroes have no souls. Father, I'm glad you insisted that we not be allowed to work our slaves on Sundays and that we give them instructions in the Christian religion."

For the next several months Father, neglecting his doctoring duties, was busy buying slaves and extending his land claims. It was during this period of time that N.W. made a great discovery.

Early one morning a man arrived on horseback. After reining in his steed he burst into N.W.'s office. "Excuse me for barging in, but my baby is due within the hour. I have to have a doctor!"

N.W. grabbed his doctor's bag. "Lead the way. I'll follow you on my horse." They traveled the back roads until they came to a rough-hewn cabin in the backwoods at Thunderbolt.

N.W. followed the man inside where his wife was already having contractions. "Quick, boil some water and begin tearing up some strips of cloth. The baby will be here soon."

The man threw his arms into the air. "I don't know a thing about birthing a baby." N.W. chuckled. "You'll be an expert by the time this is over. Just do what I tell you!"

The procedure went well, and soon a new baby girl had joined the ranks of Georgia's dwindling numbers. The man dropped his head and stammered. "Doctor Jones, I don't have any money to pay you. Can I pay you when I sell some of my produce?"

N.W. placed his arm on the man's shoulder. "You don't owe me anything. I'm happy your wife and little one are okay." N.W. picked up his satchel. "I need to be on my way. When the baby gets a little older, bring her and her mother by to see me in Savannah." The new baby's father nodded, and N.W. turned and leaped onto his horse.

All the way home N.W. dwelled on what had happened. *On my own I've delivered my first baby. Father will be thrilled. I'm thrilled!*

As the months rolled over into years, N.W.'s popularity spread rapidly throughout the colony. He went wherever he was needed on a moment's notice, often to places far removed from his office in Savannah. N.W.'s genuine interest in his patients was contagious. From far and wide people were asking for his help. At the same time N.W. felt as if he could make the journey to his sweetheart's home blindfolded. Little did he know a lurking major health problem was poised to threaten whether he'd live or die.

On a rare afternoon off N.W. went fishing. He had nabbed a big mouth bass when he suddenly felt nauseous and dizzy. His line went limp as he groped to retrieve some white oak bark from the pocket of his shirt. His hands trembled as he placed the liquid substance from the bark into his mouth. *Drat it! Now it's my turn to have the bloody flux. I know all the symptoms. How I wish Doctor Nunis were here to see me through this ordeal.*

N.W. stumbled his way back to his office, making several abrupt stops along the way. Immediately he scrounged around until he found one of Doctor Nunis' opium pills. He gulped it down, placed a damp cloth on his head, and lay down.

That's where Father found him with a raging fever. "N.W., you're coming with me to Wormsloe." N.W. protested but Father was adamant. "Stop the arguing. I've made up my mind. The change at Wormsloe will do you good."

Reluctantly, N.W. gave in to Father's wishes. Once at Wormsloe, Mother stayed busy day and night plastering his head with damp clothes and giving him cool drinks and repeated doses of quinine. Several months passed before there was any sign of improvement. Gradually the color returned to N.W.'s face, his headaches ceased, and he was no longer trotting to the privy. Still he was weak. More than a year passed before things at Wormsloe returned to normal.

Father told him, "Son, when you feel up to it I need you in Augusta. The French are working to drive a wedge between the Cherokees and us. I need you to counteract the efforts of the French."

Soon N.W. left for Augusta, where he supervised the building of log forts to protect the town. He also spent a lot of time making friends with the Cherokees. He hadn't been there long before he got a letter from Father telling him that Mother was very ill and was asking for him.

N.W. dropped what he was doing and went to his commanding officer. "Mother is critically ill, and I'm needed at home." The officer gave him leave. N.W. mounted his horse and left in a fast trot headed for Wormsloe.

It was pitch dark when N.W. arrived home. Inigo, upon hearing the neighing horse, rushed to meet his brother and to take care of his steed. N.W. went straight to Mother's side. He gently placed his arms around her. "I got here as quickly as I could. I'm so sorry you aren't feeling well."

Father, sobbing softly said, "I haven't any idea how long she lay in the garden before someone came and got me. When I got to her she was lifeless. When she finally regained consciousness the first thing she did was ask for you."

N.W. bit his lower lip as he placed his hand on her brow. He gave her a malaria tablet and a glass of water. Mary continued to put fresh cool towels on her head. Throughout the long night hours N.W. never left Mother's side. He continually squeezed her hand while telling her how much he loved her and how much he wanted to help her get well. For one brief moment her eyes fluttered. However, when N.W. tried to get her to take a sip of water her lips remained clinched. N.W. sadly shook his head, his eyes watering. "Father, nothing seems to help. I can't bear to think of losing Mother."

When she died, N.W. blamed himself. "This is all my fault. Mother contracted the bloody flux when she was taking care of me."

Father said, "N.W., Mother wouldn't want you to feel that way. Now is not the time for blame. Instead let's bond together around the love she had for each of us."

After the funeral service the family gathered at Wormsloe and began sharing their stories about Mother. Father clasped his hands together. "When London was bustling with the news of a new English colony I entertained the thought of coming here without my family." Father laughed. "Mother laid down the law, and I quickly changed my mind." His eyes roamed over the room. "When we moved into Wormsloe she was like a child with a newfound toy."

"Mrs. Jones was like a second mother to me," said John Milledge. "When Father died and I had to go to London to claim our Georgia property, your mother looked after my family." He smiled. "Then there was that time when Reverend Whitefield snatched up my brother and sister and carted them off to Bethesda."

N.W. chimed in. "Mother wasn't one to rant and rave, but the reverend's actions made her madder than a setting hen. John, Sarah's never heard about the great escape. Remind us of that story."

John leaned back. "This is the way I remember it. My sister Sarah arrived at the Blackstone cabin where I was repairing a roof, eager to tell me two men had abducted my younger brother and sister. However, Reverend Whitefield beat her to the draw. In his stern, pious voice he informed me he'd picked up my brother and sister and brought them to their new Bethesda home. I threw my hammer to the ground, missing the portly reverend by inches, and hastily descended from the roof. I screamed, 'Who gave you the right to walk onto my land and kidnap my brother and sister? I have news for you. Richard and Frances do not need Bethesda. They have a family. They'll never go hungry. As long as I have a piece of bread, so will they.'"

"Whitefield's face turned crimson, and he shook his clinched fists within a hair's breath of my face. 'They're with me now and there's nothing you can do about it.' He turned and walked away."

"I called out after him, 'Mr. Child Snatcher, we'll see about that.'"

N.W. held his hand over his mouth to keep from laughing.

"With a lot of help from your mother, James Oglethorpe, and a few others, we plotted our course. And when the reverend went on one of his money-gathering trips we reclaimed my younger brother and sister. Soon your mother arrived with new outfits of clothes and a basketful of food."

After a brief lull Mary dabbed her eyes with her handkerchief. "Mother wasn't the gossiping kind, but she got carried away with the Wesley-Sophie scandal. Every day of the big trial that rocked Savannah she made her way early to the courthouse and stayed throughout the entire session. I remember how Mother sided with Sophie. She was horrified when John Wesley refused to let Sophie, his ex-girlfriend, participate in the rite of communion. She told me, 'The reverend should be ashamed. Sophie isn't a bad person. Everyone knows John's angry because Sophie married someone other than him.'"

Up until now N.W. had said little, relishing the stories of others about his beloved mother. Sarah, his intended, never once took her eyes off her future husband as he began talking.

"Mother loved being the wife of Noble Jones and the mother of his three children. But there was always a part of her private self that remained in England. She valued her family heritage. We'd been in Savannah only a week when lightning struck a tree near the tent that held our munitions."

He caught his breath and turned to John. "I'm sure you remember the occasion. You and I were the first ones to discover the fire. With the help of the women and older men we finally got the fire doused and the ammunition moved from the big tent. While we concentrated on moving the ammunition, Mother lost the trunk her great-grandfather had made. It had been passed down through her family, and now was in her keeping. Mother treasured the horde of memories it evoked. When we discovered its charred remains, Mother was upset."

N.W. took a sip of coffee and gripped Sarah's hand. "I could tell Mother things I didn't feel free to tell anyone else. She never made fun of my fears, but she had a way of enlarging my choices."

N.W. stopped abruptly, unable to control his tears. In a little while he pulled from his tunic a tiny embroidered **W**. "Mother gave me this crest in 1739 before we left to fight the Spanish. I've kept it close to my heart all these years to remind me of her love and the heritage we share."

There was a prolonged silence until Father sidled over to Mary. "Even though you're only 22, you're now the mistress of Wormsloe. I'll get you the best of help I can find."

Mary once again dabbed her eyes. "Mother's shoes are too big for me to fill, but I'll do my best. It seems that all my life she's been preparing me for this time."

One by one N.W.'s friends began leaving. Now only N.W., Father, and Inigo remained. Father drew them into a tight circle and in a husky, strained voice said, "The days ahead will be lonely, but Mother would remind us we are family. The Lord gives and the Lord takes away. Blessed be the name of the Lord." Father and Inigo made their way to their bed space. N.W. sat in the chair close to his desk, trying to collect his thoughts.

Everyone needs someone who will mother his children and keep the family united in times of stress. I'm so fortunate my Sarah is that kind of woman.

Things in colonial Georgia never occurred in isolation. News reached Savannah that even as Mother's body was being buried, the trustees in London had turned over the colony to the British crown. Father brought the news to N.W. as he was attending a patient. His face was grim. "When you get a chance I have something you need to hear."

As soon as his patient left, N.W. hurried to hear Father's news.

"The trustees have severed all their ties with our colony. For better or worse, we'll soon be a crown colony like the other settlements in America."

N.W. raised his eyebrows. "What does this mean for us?"

"I wish I knew. It's for certain we'll be subject to a lot of changes. Let's pray they don't annex us to Carolina. Surely they'll take into account our accomplishments." Father started counting on his fingers. "We've fought a war with the Spanish, looked on as Oglethorpe returned to England, endured a month-long siege from the Bosomworths, and are holding our own with the threats of the French."

N.W. relaxed. "Hopefully they'll take into account our new slave laws and that at last our economy is showing signs of growth."

As so often happened during Georgia's colonial days, actions taken by Parliament were very slow in being implemented. Two years elapsed between the time the colony was turned over to the British crown and the arrival of John Reynolds, Georgia's first royal governor.

N.W. joined with Father and his troops to assure a royal welcome to John Reynolds, who had arrived in Savannah aboard a man-of-war in late October. Soldiers marched with precision, led by Ensn. N.W. Jones. Cannons boomed and drums rolled as the proclamation of Georgia's new status was announced in several locations. After the proclamations had been read the festive crowd joined in drinking to Governor Reynolds' health and prosperity.

It took only a few months before N.W.'s father was thoroughly disenchanted with Reynolds. As an admiral in the Royal Navy, Reynolds was used to giving orders and expecting them to be obeyed. Right away he set about ruffling feathers the wrong way and making enemies.

Father banged his fist on the kitchen table. "Governor Reynolds just fired me as senior justice of the general court, and furthermore I'm no longer a member of the Upper Council. Can you believe it?"

N.W.'s face was red with rage. "Oh, I understand all too well why he fired you. You dared to question his motives and that of his yes man, Richard Little. Parliament has yet to accept his actions." N.W. shook his fists. "If things continue like they are, we're headed for a dictatorship rather than a democracy. Our House of Commons is up in arms!"

CHAPTER 10

New Beginnings

The last of N.W.'s early morning patients had left when Father arrived. N.W. found it unnerving that Father appeared so chipper. "I don't understand. I've been bracing myself to hear your rabid reaction to being fired by Governor Reynolds. Instead, you seem happy."

Father rested his hands on his hips. "This isn't our first political storm, nor is it likely to be our last. I'm thinking that when we make known our grievances to Parliament they will act swiftly. I know as a fact that Governor Reynolds' actions run contrary to what the Crown has envisioned for Georgia."

N.W. raised his eyebrows. "Let's hope Parliament acts before he destroys our credibility with the Creek Indians. I fear our governor doesn't understand or care how fragile our Creek ties have become."

Father brushed his expansive hands across the table. "Everything you say is true. While we wait for Parliament to act, let's turn our thoughts to more positive matters."

"I'm in favor of that. What do you have in mind?"

"We need to build you a house, one befitting the stature of Savannah's leading doctor and rising statesman. Once we get that done we'll host the wedding of the century. Several years ago I did some surveying of the land adjacent to the Little Ogeechee River. The soil there is rich, and it's close but not too close to Savannah. Let's go look it over."

They closed shop and left at once. In a couple of hours they arrived at the spot Father had earlier surveyed. N.W. scratched his head. "Father, do you suppose I can get a claim to 500 acres of this prime land?"

His father twisted his hands as if he were in deep thought. Then he burst out laughing. "You can't buy it. I'm giving it to you! Share with me your ideas of what you'd like your new house to include, and we'll begin building it tomorrow."

N.W. started spilling out his long-hoarded ideas. "In addition to a large bedroom, kitchen, and parlor I'd like a library room, a corner nook for my weather instruments, and an area where Sarah can do her needle-work."

Casting his eyes toward the towering pines and hoary-haired live oaks, he placed his arm on Father's shoulder. His eyes watered. "Your gift means so much. I'm going to name our estate Lambeth, in memory of my early years near London." He paused. "Excuse me, Father. I need to stop by Sarah's on my way home. I can see her now, squealing loudly and dancing a jig."

For the following months, although political arguments grew worse instead of better, N.W. found himself less involved with politics while making frequent trips to his new homestead and keeping the path leading to Sarah Davis' house well trodden.

Summer with its sweltering heat ushered in autumn with its cooler mornings.

As the workers began putting the finishing touches on N.W.'s new home, he stopped by Wormsloe for a short visit. His sister, Mary, was retrieving a batch of rice cakes from the oven. "I'm practicing ahead of time for your wedding party," she said. "Here, have a rice cake and tell me what you think." N.W. bit into the cake. He made a mad dash for a glass of water. Sarah glanced from N.W. to Grace, the servant girl Father had given her. Then Sarah took one bite and squeaked, "My rice cakes have too much salt and no sugar! Mother is probably turning over in her grave!"

Young Grace raced to the corner of the kitchen and began wringing her hands. N.W. tapped young Grace on the shoulder. "It isn't your fault; you can't read the words sugar and salt!" Grinning mischievously, N.W. pointed to Mary. "My little sister will have to do a better job of teaching you as well as overseeing your actions."

After tossing the salty rice cakes away, a contrite Mary moaned, "Before I do another thing, Young Grace will know the words sugar and salt—and she'll know how to tell them apart." After reassuring Mary she was doing great as the new mistress of Wormsloe, N. W. left.

As the wedding grew nearer, N.W. made a list and carefully went over it with each member of his family. "Mary, you're in charge of the food and table settings. Father, you'll make sure Mary has the food she needs and lots of kitchen help. You'll also serve as our master of ceremonies."

Inigo grinned. "And what will my big brother be doing?"

N.W. smacked Inigo on his fanny. "My number-one job is to be sure all of you do your jobs. In addition to that I'll personally hand-deliver our invitations and see that we're all clothed properly. I'm putting you in charge of making sure the preacher arrives on time."

Gifts began arriving addressed to Sarah Davis and Noble Wimberly Jones, Esq.

From England came a set of blue china. At home Mary had lovingly completed the quilt Mother had started before her death. Father made the young couple a table and six chairs from mahogany. Linens, pottery, and glass stems piled up from friends and local magistrates.

The big day arrived. Although the wedding ceremonies were set for 7 o'clock in the evening, a crowd began gathering much earlier.

At 7 p.m. N.W., looking stunning in his ensign uniform, took his place at the side of Reverend Zouberbuhler. Soon he and his guests fastened their eyes toward the outer courtyard.

The loud, crisp sound of the Army buglers announced the arrival of the Davis family. The drummers added their rhythmic taps to the fanfare. N.W. looked on as Father, decked out in his captain's uniform, led Sarah's mother, dressed in a stylish soft pink dress, near the front of the gathering. As he ushered her to her seat he whispered, "It's easy to see where Sarah comes by her good looks."

Mrs. Davis smiled. "It's no wonder your son has charmed my daughter. He comes by it naturally."

Father returned to the courtyard. Again the buglers sounded and the drummers began drumming. With slow and deliberate steps, N.W.'s father ushered Sarah Davis and her father down the makeshift aisle. A knot rose in N.W.'s throat as he broke into a wide grin. *How stunning my bride looks in the white lace gown worn by her mother on her wedding day. My Sarah is so beautiful, she takes my breath away.*

When they came to the place designated for exchanging their vows Sarah's father, standing tall and looking dapper, released Sarah's hand to N.W.'s and went to take his place by his wife.

Once N.W. and Sarah had exchanged their vows their friends began gathering around the tables laden with venison, fish, turkey, pork, and beef and an abundance of corn, rice, carrots, and sweet potatoes. N.W. and Sarah moved among their friends, making each of them feel welcomed. Gradually the food area was cleared, and the plucking of violins signaled it was time to dance.

N.W. bowed to Sarah. "Hello, beautiful. Can I have this dance with you?"

Sarah curtsied. "Yes, my handsome husband, you may."

N.W. whirled Sarah around the dance floor, and soon the floor was jammed with couples eager to celebrate. N.W. maneuvered Sarah onto the piazza, a screened porch, and whispered, "Help me keep an eye on John and his cronies. I know he's not going to let this event end without playing some sort of dirty trick. Look at him! I can see the devilment oozing out his eyes."

Sarah laughed and twisted N.W.'s nose. "Maybe you can outsmart him."

"I haven't a chance. He's probably been scheming for months."

"Look!" said Sarah. "John just made a sign to his buddies. They're leaving."

"Stay here," said N.W. "I'll explain our departure to Father. If we're lucky, we can foil their plans."

N.W. with Sarah in front of him on his horse took all the back paths to his new home.

As he struggled to open their front door, he clinched his jaws. "Sarah! John and his friends got here ahead of us. Those rascals have padlocked our door!"

Then N.W. relaxed and pressed his hands against his chin. "What they don't know is, I've a secret entrance. Honey, stay here and I'll open the door from the inside."

Shortly N.W. opened the front door, ready to sweep Sarah in his arms and swish her over the threshold. Sarah had vanished! N.W. stomped his foot. "Alright, John Milledge. Enough is enough!" he shouted. His eye caught the trembling bushes to his right. He plunged into the bush, retrieved his giggling wife while shooing John and his friends away.

N.W. pretended to be upset. "Alright, alright," said a grim-faced John. "We're leaving. My plan would have worked if you didn't have such a giggly wife."

"Sarah, shame on you! "said N.W. "You knew all about John's plan, didn't you?"

Sarah rolled her eyes. She teased, "A wee bit of excitement never hurt anyone. Honey, pick me up. I'm ready to be carried across the threshold."

In the weeks and months ahead, marital bliss and doctoring the sick and continuous wranglings with Governor Reynolds filled N.W.'s landscape.

When Father arrived at work one morning N.W. ushered him to a chair. "Before our office becomes filled with sick people we need to talk"

"What's on your mind?

"How do you feel about becoming a grandfather?"

Father hopped up. "That's terrific! Do I dance a jig now or wait until the little tyke arrives?"

"Wait a bit. Please sit back down. I have something else to talk over with you. As you know, we've spent more than eight years together in our apprenticeship and . . ."

Father pushed his right hand forward. "Stop right there. It's past time for you to open your own office. Long ago you absorbed all I know." He paused before continuing. "Besides, I need all the time I can get to do battle with our dreadful royal governor."

With a gleam in his eyes N.W. said, "Go to it, Father! Warn the governor that he's playing with fire with his overtures to the Bosomworths." Letting out a deep, satisfying sigh, N.W. added, "I'll keep you posted on the arrival of your first grandchild. He's destined to bring all of us great joy."

The months passed swiftly. Sarah went into labor and N.W. delivered their firstborn, a beautiful baby girl. With haste one of N.W.'s servants galloped away to share the good news with the child's grandparents. Soon Father, Mary, Inigo, and Sarah's parents joined the happy parents at Lambeth to usher in the next generation of the Jones clan.

Less than two weeks later Father stopped by N.W.'s office, bubbly and chipper.

N.W. stared at Father and began probing. "OK, out with it. I haven't seen you this carefree since the arrival of John Reynolds. Have you found a pot of gold?"

"What I've found means more than a pot of gold. Finally Parliament has responded to our complaints about Reynolds. They've called for our royal governor to vacate his office in Georgia at once, and it's rumored our new governor will be Henry Ellis."

N.W. raised his eyebrows. "Ellis? Is that good or bad?"

"Make up your own mind. My sources in Carolina tell me he's already in Charleston, and in contrast to Reynolds he's someone with intelligence, tact, sensitivity, wit, and political ability."

Within a month Henry Ellis arrived at Savannah, with 90 percent of the people on hand to give him a royal welcome. The people fired off their few pieces of artillery, built a huge bonfire, and tossed an effigy of William Little—the friend and "yes man" of Governor Reynolds—into the blaze. The celebration continued all night and into the wee hours of morning.

The next day N.W. listened as Governor Ellis held up his hands to quiet the noisy crowd. "Don't let the likes of Mr. Reynolds and Mr. Little upset you. They're the least of my worries. I'm going to teach you how to govern yourselves. How does that sound?"

The crowd broke out into a thunderous applause.

"The first thing I'm going to do is adjoin the current council until Reynolds and his ilk leave for England. Meanwhile I'm calling a meeting of the old council that served under the trustees."

N.W. extended his hand, introducing himself. "Governor Ellis, I'm N.W. Jones, son of Noble Jones. I want to personally thank you for your healing words. Before you came Father was constantly arguing with Mr. Reynolds. He believes you will be a fair administrator. Tell me more about your idea of dividing our colony into eight parishes."

"The people of a given parish will elect their representative, and he in turn will have a seat on our Common House council. Every parish will have one vote." Ellis smiled. "How does that sound to you?"

N.W. chuckled. "I'm all for it. It won't stop our arguing, but at least no one can say nobody listens. I'll be happy to sponsor your proposal."

⸺✦⸺

Lambeth, the country estate of N.W. Jones, had long ceased being simply a house. It had become a home, a haven of family love and joy. Likewise it was a place where extended family and guests always found a warm welcome.

Father had arrived early, bringing with him one of his carved walking stick horses for little Sarah, now two and managing to make her presence known.

When Governor Ellis rapped on the door N.W., with tiny Sarah hoisted on his hip said, "Welcome to Lambeth, Governor Ellis. Sarah and I are honored to have you. Do come in."

Father motioned for him to have a seat near him. "Henry, I hope you don't get confused by our multiple Sarahs. N.W.'s mother was named Sarah. He married Sarah Davis, and they've chosen to name their first-born Sarah.

Governor Ellis laughed. "Now that we have that matter straightened out, tell me what is that delicious aroma coming from your kitchen."

Nancy, their house servant said, "That's deer meat simmering in curry spices from India. I hope you're ready to eat. She patted N.W. on his shoulder, saying, "Master Jones just picks at his food and eats like a bird."

After dinner the men gathered in the parlor while Sarah enticed little Sarah to go with her to the nursery.

"Father, Governor Ellis tells me he wants us to come up with a budget, to pass legislation to clarify our land titles and to define our Indian trade regulations. Why don't you spearhead a proposed budget in the Upper House? When you send it to us in the House of Commons I feel certain I can get it passed by my peers."

"N.W.," said Governor Ellis, "do you agree we can never get the Creek Indians to side with us if we continue to ignore Mary Bosomworth's land claims?"

N.W. nodded his head. "When we landed at Savannah in 1733 it was Mary who convinced her fellow Creeks that we wanted to be friends. Time and again she exposed herself to personal danger to get us the support of her Creek nation. I well remember the occasion when Chief Tomochichi deeded her Ossabaw, Sapelo, and St. Catherine's Islands."

Father entered the conversation. "Mary changed greatly after she married Thomas Bosomworth. She began drinking heavily and making irrational threats against our colony. On one occasion she came with 700 braves and threatened to burn down our town if we ignored her land claims."

The governor listened intently and spoke softly. "I've been working for several months with Mary and Thomas Bosomworth. I'm determined to bring their land settlement to a satisfactory conclusion." He cast his eyes toward Father. "Regardless of how worthless her husband might be, it's wrong to mistreat our friends. I'm convinced Mary has befriended Georgia time and again. We're giving the Bosomworths St. Catherine's Island and paying them a lump sum for Ossabaw and Sapelo Islands. They've agreed to our settlement."

N.W. smiled broadly. "That makes me very happy, and I agree with you that it's the right thing to do." N.W. was grateful that for once Father didn't argue about the governor's decision.

"Governor, before you leave I'd like for you to see my little weather station."

"I was hoping you'd share your findings with me. Your father has told me about your interest in the way climate affects our health. I find that fascinating. Daily at noon I record the temperature here in Savannah and make a weekly report to Lord Halifax at the Royal Academy."

N.W.'s eyes lit up. "Ah, so that explains your noontime walks under that big parasol with a dangling thermometer."

"Yes, after a brief walk I return to my room and record Savannah's temperature for the day. It's part of a continuing study I'm conducting."

N.W. nodded his head. "I'm convinced weather affects our health. I've kept a record every day for years of our temperatures."

Governor Ellis wiped his forehead and grinned. "Tell me how you've survived this dreadful heat. I've been to many hot spots around the world, but none of them compares with Georgia. Mercy me! This heat leaves me whimpering like a stray kitten."

The months unfolded into years and at last the struggling colony of Georgia, under Governor Ellis, began to prosper. N.W. Jones with a loving wife, an adoring toddler, and another child on the way was enjoying domestic tranquility. There was a growing demand for his medical services, and the up-and-coming young adults of the colony curried his political approval.

News that Governor Ellis, because of ill health, was leaving Georgia occurred at the same time N.W. was coming to terms with a deep personal loss.

N.W. kept his worries to himself. He teased, "Sarah, if you get any bigger, we might have a baby elephant."

Sarah grimaced, "I know. I feel like I weigh a ton!"

N.W. reached over and stole a kiss. "Darling, you won't have to wait much longer. Everything is ready. Little Sarah has gone to be with your mother and Sue, our midwife, is now living in our guest room."

Suddenly Sarah grabbed her stomach. "Whew! That felt like someone stabbed me with a knife."

N.W. rapped on Sue's door. "Come quickly! Sarah is having birth pangs." N.W. followed every move she made as she began helping Sarah position herself best for the delivery. Soon the pain grew intense and Sarah was screaming, her brow covered with sweat beads. There was one final scream, and N.W. went to work bringing forth a tiny boy from Sarah's womb while Sarah lay limp as a dishrag.

N.W. spanked the baby's bottom, but he got only a whimper. N.W. emerged from his office-at-home as if he'd been grappling with a tiger. His tear-stained face was red, and his drained voice husky as he cuddled Sarah in his arms. "Honey, I did everything I knew and still I lost our precious baby."

"I know. I know," whispered Sarah.

N.W. sobbed. "I've brought life and health to so many. But when it comes to saving the life of my own son I'm helpless."

He watched as Sarah's eyes roamed over the tiny outfits laid out in joyous anticipation.

Sarah gulped as she fondled one of the outfits. "I guess we won't be needing these anytime soon."

She caressed N.W.'s cheek. Don't fret, Sweetheart. We're young and we'll try again."

With the help of their household servants they buried their baby on the grounds of Lambeth.

Sarah held onto N.W. "Honey, please send word to Mother about our loss. Tell her to come quickly and to bring little Sarah home."

"I'll do that right away and let Father also share our sorrow." N.W. had no sooner sent his servants to notify their parents until there came a rapping at their door. A young adult stood in the doorway. "Doctor Jones, come quickly. My wife is about to give birth."

N.W. was about to excuse himself when Sarah urged, "Go. They need you. Nancy will take care of us until you return."

N.W. kissed Sarah on the cheek, wiped off his pocket lancet, and left immediately.